Get a Life

clearwater crossing

Get a Life

laura peyton roberts

BANTAM BOOKS
NEW YORK • TORONTO • LONDON • SYDNEY • AUCKLAND

RL 5.8, age 12 and up
GET A LIFE
A Bantam Book/April 1998

ISBN 0-553-57118-4

Published simultaneously in the United States and Canada.

Bantam Books are published by Bantam Books, a division of Bantam
Doubleday Dell Publishing Group, Inc. Its trademark, consisting of the
words "Bantam Books" and the portrayal of a rooster, is Registered in
U.S. Patent and Trademark Office and in other countries. Marca Reg-
istrada. Bantam Books, 1540 Broadway, New York, New York 10036.

PRINTED IN THE UNITED STATES OF AMERICA

OPM   10 9 8 7 6 5 4 3 2 1

For my parents, with love

One

"Go, Wildcats," Mrs. Wilson concluded, dropping the principal's announcement onto her desk.

Jenna Conrad watched the paper flutter down to the scratched Formica surface with an identical flutter in her excited heart. Here she was, starting her very first class as a junior, and the year ahead already seemed loaded with promise. She and her best friend, Peter Altmann, had arrived at school early to say hello to people they hadn't seen much over the summer, and the whole campus was buzzing with first-day energy. Everyone was running around greeting old friends and comparing notes on their vacations, and even the kids Jenna had seen every week at church looked different that morning in their first-day outfits.

To top things off, it was Spirit Day. There was a long-standing tradition at CCHS that on the first day of school all the members of the sports teams wore their jerseys, and the cheerleaders modeled the year's new uniforms. There was so much green

1

and gold on campus that the school felt like a theme park.

"I hope you'll all go to the carnival," Mrs. Wilson told her students, opening a brand-new roll book. "It's certainly a worthy cause."

Jenna heard the teacher's words at half-volume, as an undercurrent to the other thoughts racing through her head. Of course she'd go to the carnival and, knowing her family, her parents and sisters would probably go too. But at that moment she was far more interested in the fact that Miguel del Rios, the guy she'd had a crush on for the last two years, was sitting in the row right next to her.

"Carver," Mrs. Wilson droned. "Conrad . . ."

"Here!" Jenna answered.

"del Rios . . ."

"Here." His voice was deep for a high-school guy. Jenna risked a furtive peek at his profile, taking in the cool white smile, the summer-tanned cheeks, and the wavy dark hair that barely brushed his collar. Miguel's eyes were dark, too—a clear deep brown the color of Coke over ice.

Jenna vividly remembered the first time she'd ever seen him. Her freshman gym class had been swimming lackluster laps in the indoor pool, and the teacher had just dismissed them. Everyone climbed out onto the deck and ran for the locker room, but Jenna lagged behind, unable to wait another second before peeling off the swimming cap

2

that was cutting an angry pink trench in her fore-head. She'd stayed to squeeze the water out of her long brown hair, and that was when she'd spotted Miguel coming out with the rest of the water polo team, dressed to swim in a green Speedo and white water polo cap.

There was something about his face that had caught her attention immediately. Even in the middle of that rowdy, wisecracking group, Miguel had stood apart from the other guys, as if he were holding himself inside somehow. She'd stood there watching, mesmerized, while he'd pushed his way to the poolside with his friends, and by the time his long, arcing entry dive cut the surface of the water, Jenna had made up her mind. Somehow, someday, she wanted to know Miguel del Rios.

Following up on that decision had turned out to be harder than Jenna had imagined. For one thing, Miguel's reserve made her shy about approaching him. For another, that same reserve gave him an air of mystery that drove even the most popular girls at school crazy. Jenna would never follow him to his classes or wait for him in the parking lot the way some of them did, but she *had* developed a secret habit of looking for him in the crowd whenever there was an assembly or a football game.

"Hey, Jenna!" Cyn Girard whispered urgently from the row on Jenna's left. "Can I borrow a pencil?"

Jenna jumped, startled. The roll call had come to an end. "Sure," she whispered back, picking up her backpack and riffling through the detritus at the bottom. Jenna had known Cyn forever, and the girl's modus operandi never varied—coming to class prepared was simply not her style.

"Here." Jenna handed over a freshly sharpened pencil, knowing she'd never see it again.

"You're a lifesaver!" Cyn whispered gratefully. "How do you remember this stuff, anyway?"

"I think most people would agree that pencils are pretty basic equipment," Jenna teased. "Especially on the first day of school." She didn't mind, though. She always kept a few extras in her pack in case someone needed one.

"All right, everybody," said Mrs. Wilson, raising her voice above the growing chatter. "I'm going to ask Hugh and John to pass out those textbooks, and then we'll get right to work." There was a unanimous groan as the teacher pointed toward several stacks of heavy, dog-eared geometry books on a table at the front of the room.

Mrs. Wilson smiled good-humoredly. "You've all had too much fun this summer—*that's* the problem. Well, don't worry. I'm back on the job now." The groan echoed around the room again, this time accompanied by reluctant smiles as Hugh and John got up to pass out books.

"Do you know Kurt Englbehrt?" Cyn asked Jenna in the noisy interval that followed.

"I know who he is, but I don't really know him. Do you?"

"Yeah, a little. The guy's a total babe. At least he used to be—he didn't look so great the last time I saw him." A shadow crossed Cyn's face and she unconsciously tucked her auburn hair behind both ears.

"What's wrong with him?" Jenna asked curiously. "I mean, what exactly is leukemia?"

"Cancer," Cyn answered, a shudder in her voice. "It gets in your bone marrow somehow."

"Oh, Cyn!" Jenna felt a shiver run all the way down both arms. It seemed inconceivable that someone so young—one of her own *classmates*— could get cancer. "Is he very sick? I thought Principal Kelly's announcement said Kurt was here at school."

Cyn nodded. "He is, but he's been in and out of the hospital all summer for chemotherapy and radiation. I saw him and his girlfriend, Dana, at the mall last week and *I* thought he looked scary, but they both think he's better. They're hoping he's close to remission."

"Remission?"

"In remission, the cancer disappears. Sometimes it comes back later, and then they have to try more treatment. But sometimes it just goes away."

"And they think that will happen to Kurt? Thank God!"

"Yeah. Whatever." Cyn smiled skeptically. "But I think his doctors had more to do with it."

"Here you go, ladies," a sarcastic male voice interrupted. "Enjoy." Heavy geometry books fell onto Jenna's and Cyn's desks with twin thuds as John passed up their aisle.

"Gee, thanks," said Cyn, making a face.

Jenna turned around in her chair and flipped idly through her textbook, not really seeing the endless pages of geometry problems or the scribbled notes penciled in the margins. Her mind was still on Kurt.

How awful to be so sick! she thought. She tried to imagine herself or one of her sisters with a serious disease, but she couldn't. It seemed impossible, unreal. *Nothing that bad has ever happened to my family*, she realized, surprised now that she'd never thought about it before. *We've always been pretty happy. Of course, having four sisters still living at home isn't exactly a picnic. . . .* But to have one of her sisters get as sick as Kurt Englbehrt was, was too horrible to even think about.

Jenna's thoughts returned to the carnival. She would definitely go, she decided, and she'd pray for Kurt every night. Not only that, but if she talked to her mom about it, Mrs. Conrad might ask Reverend Thompson to take up a special collection for the Englbehrt family. Having a plan made Jenna feel better, and with a feeling of renewed optimism she turned her text to the page number Mrs. Wilson was writing on the blackboard.

"Psst, Miguel! What page are we on?" Jenna heard Chelsea Stephens whisper from the seat directly behind his. Jenna glanced over to see the pretty girl leaning forward on her desk, trying to get his attention. "I can barely see the board from way back here," she added, playing for sympathy.

Miguel turned around in his chair. "Page fourteen," he said quietly. "Maybe you should move to a seat closer to the front."

His voice gave away nothing, but Jenna thought she saw a flicker of amusement in his eyes—just enough to convince her he knew that Chelsea was faking her sudden blindness.

Chelsea squirmed uncomfortably. "Oh, uh, that's okay. I can read it if I squint."

"You ought to get your eyes checked," Miguel persisted. "Maybe you need glasses."

The mere mention of glasses made Chelsea look so horrified that Jenna had to stifle a giggle.

"*No!* I mean, I'm sure I don't. I'll, uh, get used to seeing from back here. It'll be fine."

Miguel raised one heavy eyebrow, then turned his attention back to the teacher. Jenna, meanwhile, still struggled not to burst out laughing. If the first half hour indicated anything, it was that her junior year was going to be incredible. She could barely wait to see Peter at lunchtime and find out if he was as excited as she was.

Not that she was going to tell him about Miguel. She'd never even told Peter she had a crush on anyone, let alone mentioned the incredible, inexplicable effect Miguel had on her. Peter Altmann might have been her best friend since sixth grade, but he was still a guy. He wouldn't understand.

"*Melanie!* Melanie Andrews! Marry me or I'll kill myself!"

Melanie slowed her steps and glanced toward the group of rowdy basketball players on the lawn in front of the high school. Senior Ricky Black immediately fell to his knees on the steaming emerald grass, hamming it up while his teammates egged him on.

"I can't eat. I can't sleep. I'll *die*, I tell you." He made this declaration in the most pitiful voice imaginable, his hands clasped and stretched out in front of him.

"We can only hope," Melanie teased, rolling her light green eyes. Ricky was known as the team clown, but this latest effort seemed more like an incredibly bad audition for the school drama club.

"Ooh! That's cold!" John Killian exclaimed, smacking his buddy hard between the shoulder blades. Ricky clutched convulsively at his heart and fell face-forward on the grass in the most fake, yet protracted, death scene that Melanie had ever witnessed.

"Bye-bye, Ricky," she said, when his body finally stopped twitching. "Nice knowing ya." Ricky's friends responded with jeers and laughter as Melanie tossed her head and resumed her saunter across campus.

"Can you believe those guys?" she asked her fellow cheerleaders, acutely aware of the way her short pleated skirt switched at the tops of her tan legs and her sun-streaked blond hair bounced behind her in a ponytail tied with a broad green ribbon. "They never give it a rest."

Lou Anne Simmons managed to walk, shrug, and touch up her mascara all at the same time. "Forget about *them*. Can you believe that horrible Mrs. Gregor? What kind of sadist assigns homework on the first day of school?"

"You have *homework*?" Angela Maldonado repeated, appalled. "None of my teachers made us do *anything*."

"Of course not!" Lou Anne exclaimed. "No one does anything on the first day of school. It's practically a law or something."

"Someone should have told Mrs. Gregor." The weight of the heavy history text in Melanie's tote bag was making the canvas handles cut creases in her hand. Normally she would have worn a backpack,

9

but not today—not on her very first chance to wear her brand-new cheerleader's uniform.

"Isn't Gregor about a hundred years old?" Vanessa Winters, the senior squad captain, asked in a bored tone of voice. "Maybe they told her and she already forgot."

Lou Anne laughed loudly, sucking up. "Probably."

Melanie had actually kind of liked cranky, independent Mrs. Gregor, but she had to admit that she wasn't any more thrilled about reading the history chapters than Lou Anne was.

"Hey, Melanie! Wait up!" a male voice boomed suddenly. Melanie and her friends turned to see Jesse Jones, CCHS's new football stud extraordinaire, hurrying toward them, a couple of teammates in tow.

"Ooh, Melanie," Angela teased. "I think someone likes you."

Melanie smiled noncommittally and shrugged. "So many men . . . ," she said with a sigh.

"Don't pay him any attention," Vanessa advised in a low, guarded voice. "The guy's a total flirt."

Melanie didn't reply as the four of them waited for Jesse to catch up. Jesse Jones was a very good-looking guy—tall and lean with light brown hair and intense blue eyes under low, straight brows. He'd transferred to Clearwater Crossing from a school in California the semester before, but Melanie had met him during the summer, when the football team and the cheerleaders had held meeting after meeting to plan the upcoming carnival. And Vanessa was right—he *was* a flirt. Still, Melanie wasn't exactly inexperienced in that area herself. She could handle him.

"Hey, Melanie," Jesse said, his voice full of studied nonchalance as he reached her group. "What are you doing?"

Melanie regarded him coolly. "Walking."

Jesse's buddies snickered and Jesse flinched. "Obviously," he said, a little less confidently. "I meant, what are you doing this afternoon?"

"That depends on what you have in mind," she told him, letting the invitation dangle.

Vanessa's pained groan was drowned out by the hoots and laughter of Jesse's two companions.

"Way to go, man!" yelped Gary Baldwin, slapping Jesse on the back. The other guy, a kid whose name Melanie could never remember, tried to high-five Jesse from his other side.

"Will you two knock it off?" Jesse snapped irritably. "What do you say we drive around a little?" he asked, turning to Melanie. "Maybe head out to the lake?"

Lou Anne giggled and Jesse shot her a lethal look. The lake was the designated makeout spot—Melanie had to give the guy points for trying.

"You driving that pretty red BMW today?" she asked.

"You bet." Jesse puffed out his chest.

"Then you can drive me home. But after that I'm busy."

With a quick wave good-bye to her friends, Melanie struck off across the lawn in the direction of the student parking lot, Jesse on her heels. The grass beneath her Nikes was thick and springy, and it was late enough in the year that the humidity had backed off. The long Missouri summer was giving way to fall, turning the sky over the Ozarks a hazy, purplish blue.

"Here it is," Jesse announced as they reached his car. "I washed it yesterday." The pristine BMW sparkled in the afternoon sunlight, and Jesse hurried to open its passenger door for Melanie. She climbed in cautiously, testing the temperature of the black leather against the backs of her bare thighs before settling down into the seat.

"Are you sure you don't want to cruise the lake on the way home?" Jesse asked as he buckled his seat belt. The expression on his face was smug, confident.

"In your dreams," Melanie returned sweetly.

Jesse winced, then laughed, then started the engine. It was only a game, and they both knew it.

If I said "Yeah, let's go," he'd probably have an accident, Melanie thought, smiling to herself as they pulled out onto the roadway.

Melanie was used to guys making passes. She was

only fifteen, but the boys had started lining up in kindergarten. It was frequently annoying—for instance, when some lovestruck loser took to following her around and calling her house at all hours—but at other times it was pretty convenient. Today, for example, a little low-key flirting was getting her a ride straight to her doorstep instead of a long, sweaty trip on that hot, smelly bus.

"So, are you looking forward to school this year?" Jesse asked.

"I guess. You?"

"Are you kidding? I'm on varsity now. Besides, I think we're going to regionals this year."

Melanie nodded and tried to look interested. Now that she was a cheerleader, she had to at least *pretend* to care about sports. "If we beat Red River," she said dutifully.

"Oh, we'll beat 'em," Jesse predicted confidently. "You heard it here first."

They drove in silence after that, Melanie relaxing gradually into the hot leather seat. The warm air pouring through her open window flowed over her bare arms and ruffled the stray strands of hair around her face, and Melanie breathed in deeply, taking in the mixed odors of livestock and dying leaves.

"Turn here," she said after a while. "My house is down at the end."

Jesse steered the BMW around the corner and

along the short private road. The Andrewses' place sat regally at the dead end, towering above the surrounding oaks, sycamores, and dogwoods like a glass-and-concrete castle.

"What a wild house," Jesse said as he pulled up the driveway. "It looks like something you'd see in California instead of way out here in Misery."

Melanie chose to ignore the insult to her native state. "My mother helped the architect design it. It's all custom," she explained, letting herself out of the car.

"Hey!" Jesse called quickly, before she could shut the door. "Why don't I come in for a while? You can give me the grand tour."

"Maybe some other time. I have things to do now."

"Do them later," Jesse suggested.

Melanie shook her head, an easy smile on her lips. "Thanks for the ride. I'll see you in school tomorrow."

Eventually Jesse drove off, and Melanie let herself inside. The immense, two-story entry hall was cool and silent. Melanie stooped to the gray marble floor, collected the mail scattered under the mail slot, and shuffled through it listlessly: bill, bill, junk mail, another bill, something that might be a check. Putting the envelopes on the antique hall table for her father, she climbed the curving open staircase to her room.

14

Her mother had always said that the staircase was the showpiece of the house, but Melanie barely noticed the bare expanse of raw concrete wall on her right or the dramatic drop to the formal living room on her left as she trotted up the smooth marble stairs. Reaching her enormous bedroom suite, she dropped her heavy tote bag gratefully, crossed to her walk-in closet, and threw its double doors open wide.

If the staircase was the showpiece of the house, then the closet was the showpiece of Melanie's room. It was big enough to park two cars in, for one thing, and completely fitted out with specially designed rods, shelves, drawers, and shoe compartments. Melanie stepped inside, kicked off her shoes, and removed the sleeveless white top of her cheerleader's outfit.

"Go, Wildcats," she murmured with a smile, running a hand over the bold green-and-gold CCHS sewn to its fabric and remembering the day in April that she'd tried out for cheerleading. She was the only freshman ever to have made the cut—most didn't even try—and the gym had erupted into utter pandemonium when her name had been announced. She was already one of the most popular, most talked-about girls at school. Becoming a sophomore cheerleader had lifted her to the status of legend.

Melanie removed a padded satin hanger from

one of the rods and hung up her top, then slipped out of the green-and-gold pleated skirt and put that on a hanger as well. The skirt slid into place next to the matching sweater—the one she'd wear when cold weather came—and the uniform sank back into line with the rest of Melanie's expensive, extensive wardrobe.

But Melanie stayed stuck on the spot where she stood, her eyes roaming her closet without really seeing. It was always like this when she was alone. Her mind would start to wander, to turn backward. . . .

Spinning around, Melanie hurried out of the closet, still in her underwear. Her room was immaculate, she noticed distractedly—the cleaning woman, Mrs. Murphy, must have come. All Melanie's books were perfectly aligned on their shelves and her childhood doll collection was dusted and primped. The watercolor landscape she'd painted under her mother's patient tutelage lay brilliant behind its bright glass, and the vertical blinds hanging at her wide picture windows had been opened to their limits, exposing the front two acres of the Andrewses' property.

Melanie's eyes dropped slowly from the familiar rolling land with its dense green stands of hardwood trees to the thick white carpet beneath her stockinged feet. It was spotless, like freshly vacuumed snow. She stood there a long time, mesmerized. There was always a moment like this—a quiet, frozen moment just before she let herself remember.

She stood there motionless as her mind nudged, then prodded, then tore into the scarred old wound inside it. The familiar pain welled up like nausea, building a lump in her throat. Melanie welcomed the pain, leaned into it. With closed eyes she let the past wash over her until her knees gave out and she collapsed facedown on her pale pink bedspread.

Then at last came the sobs, in great, racking gasps.

Two

"Jenna!" Sarah bellowed. "It's for you!" The announcement was punctuated by the sound of the front door slamming.

"Who is it?" Jenna called back. "I'm up to my elbows in soapsuds here." She abandoned the half-washed dinner dishes and reached for a towel, but she'd barely begun drying her hands when her youngest sister, ten-year-old Sarah, appeared in the kitchen, followed by Jenna's friend Peter.

"Gee, don't get all dolled up for *me*," Peter teased as Jenna wiped drifts of bubbles off her forearms. Jenna grinned and flicked the last hunk of suds at him with a practiced forefinger.

"Hey!" He ducked, but too slowly, and Jenna's aim was perfect. The quivering white glob landed triumphantly in Peter's dark blond hair. He wiped at it, making a face as the bubbles squished into his scalp.

"She shoots, she scores!" Jenna crowed, laughing.

"You're dangerous," Peter grumbled.

"You started it."

"I'm not finishing those dishes for you, Jenna," Jenna's sister Maggie warned from the other side of the sink. Her freckled face was crumpled with annoyance. "It's my night to dry, and that's all I'm doing."

"No one's asking you to do any extra work, Maggie," Jenna said, rolling her eyes for Peter's benefit. "I wouldn't dream of it."

Jenna and Maggie shared a room, so there was always more tension between them than between Jenna and her other four sisters. Of course Mary Beth was away at her second year of college now, so there was no tension there. Jenna wished that her next oldest sister, Caitlin, would get off her duff and move out too so that Jenna could have her own room. It wasn't fair for Caitlin to keep hanging around taking up space now that she'd graduated from high school. If she wasn't going to college, the least she could do was get a job and find an apartment somewhere.

"Don't act so smart, Jenna," said Maggie, glancing self-consciously at Peter. "I have a lot to do to get ready for school tomorrow, that's all."

"Like what? Writing 'Mrs. Scott Jenner' all over the *rest* of your notebooks?"

Maggie blushed so furiously that Jenna belatedly wished she'd kept that particular discovery to herself. That was the problem with sharing a room—a

19

person ended up knowing way too much about her roommate. Enough to be deadly, in fact.

"So, Maggie," Peter broke in hurriedly, his tone soothing. "How do you like eighth grade so far? How does it feel to be in the grade all the other kids look up to?"

Maggie shot Jenna one last evil look, then smiled shyly at Peter. "It's okay. It's better than being in seventh."

"I heard that!" seventh-grader Allison yelled from the dining room, where she was polishing the enormous wooden dining table. "Seventh-graders rule!"

"No, fifth!" Sarah declared, skipping madly around the kitchen. "Fifth-graders rule!"

"Let's go out to the porch," Jenna told Peter, heading for the back door. "We aren't going to get any peace in here."

"Jenna! I'm *not*—" Maggie began irately.

"I'll finish the dishes later, all right? I'll even *dry* them for you. Come on, Peter," she added. "Let's get out of here."

The back door banged shut behind them, blocking out most of the noise from inside, as Jenna and Peter stepped out into the cool evening air. "What a zoo!" Jenna sighed, savoring the comparative quiet on the porch.

Peter smiled. "You know I like your sisters."

"I like them too. Preferably from a distance." She

laughed as she said it, though, and they both knew she was kidding. The Conrad family was as tight as the lid on a five-year-old jar of molasses.

Jenna walked to the edge of the porch and dropped cross-legged into a large, old-fashioned porch swing, motioning for Peter to sit beside her. "So what are you doing here, anyway? I didn't expect to see you again until tomorrow."

Peter's tall, skinny frame folded up like a lawn chair as he lowered himself into the swing. "Everything was so crazy at lunch today—I meant to ask you something, but I forgot."

Jenna nodded expectantly.

"You know that carnival they're having at school for Kurt Englbehrt this weekend? I'm going to volunteer to help, and I was wondering if you'd want to volunteer with me."

"Aren't you meeting with the Junior Explorers this Saturday?" Junior Explorers was a club Peter and a college-age friend, Chris Hobart, had started for underprivileged children. The group met at the local park every Saturday to play games, learn arts and crafts, and just generally have some fun. During the summer they went on field trips and to summer camp. Jenna helped out off and on, whenever Peter needed her, but Peter had barely missed a Saturday for the last two years.

"I called Chris and asked him to cover for me. I

don't know Kurt that well, but I've had him in a couple of classes. He's a nice guy, Jenna."

"Yeah, I want to help out too. I'm glad you reminded me, in fact, because I meant to ask my mom if Reverend Thompson would take up a special collection at church this Sunday."

"Oh, sure. Now that your mom's the choir director, you have all the good connections," Peter teased.

"Very funny." Jenna stuck out her tongue. "You're just jealous because you couldn't carry a tune in a bucket." It was a sad-but-true fact that Peter was completely tone-deaf.

"I couldn't carry a tune in an armored vehicle," Peter said ruefully. "It's hopeless. I'm doomed to forever bask in the reflected glory of my friend Jenna, the soloist."

"You goof," Jenna giggled, smacking him playfully in the arm. Peter was always saying stuff like that.

"So what about the carnival?" he asked. "Do you want to do it or not?"

"Of course!" She thought about going straight in to tell her parents, then remembered that her chores were still unfinished. "But right now I'd better get back to those dishes. Should we meet at the same place for lunch tomorrow?"

"Okay." Peter smiled, flashing the even white teeth that Jenna had long considered his best feature. "You know, I really think school will be great this year. The junior class rules!"

"My sisters are a bad influence on you," Jenna told him, laughing.

But after Peter had left for home, Jenna remembered his words. It *was* going to be a great year. She had everything to look forward to—school, family, friends, church. Not to mention the little matter of Miguel del Rios being in her homeroom! Jenna's lips curled into a satisfied smile as she finished the dinner dishes.

Miguel del Rios. If only she could tell Peter!

"Don't forget," Courtney Bell said on Tuesday, peeling a layer of plastic wrap off her sandwich with short red fingernails. "If I win, you have to give me the dress you wore to the Spring Fling last year."

"All *right*," snapped Nicole. "I said I would, didn't I?"

"Yes, and now I'm just reminding you." Courtney's voice was calm, unruffled. "I have big plans for that dress," she added, waggling her auburn eyebrows.

"Whatever."

Nicole Brewster wished like crazy that she'd never made that bet with Courtney in the first place. After all, who really cared who got asked out first? Nicole glanced at her smirking best friend, annoyed once again by her own stupidity. Competing with Courtney for the first date of the school year was nothing but a ton more pressure she didn't need. Besides, the way Courtney was dressing to thrill gave her a totally unfair advantage.

Over the summer, Nicole had pored over every fashion-and-diet magazine she could get her hands on. She'd lost ten pounds and her wardrobe had definitely improved as a result, but she still couldn't compete with Courtney in the sex-appeal department. Courtney had serious cleavage, for one thing. Not only that, but everyone said her red hair meant she was passionate—a rumor Courtney herself had probably started.

"Why don't you just take the dress now and quit hounding me?" Nicole asked grumpily.

"Attitude check!" Courtney returned, unperturbed. "Oops. Yours sucks."

Nicole grimaced. "I know. I'm sorry. I'll tell you what—let's go shopping after school today. I'll figure out which bracelet you have to buy me when *I* win our bet."

"Dream on!" Courtney hooted. "As far as I'm concerned, you can pick out solid diamonds."

Nicole knew her friend was only bluffing, but she still felt certain that Courtney would win the bet. It wasn't that her own case was so *totally* hopeless compared to Courtney's; it was simply that the deck was stacked against her. The problem was that Nicole was keeping a big, big secret: she didn't want to go out with just *anyone*—she wanted to go out with Jesse Jones.

Ever since Jesse had transferred into her English class the year before, Nicole had been obsessed with the cute football player from California. She'd done everything she could think of to get his attention, but so far all her efforts had come to nothing. Well, not exactly *nothing*. At least he knew who she was now, and he'd say hi if he saw her in the hall or someplace. But a girl could only live so long off the thrill of the random nod or wave. Nicole wanted more. Much more.

I'll be Jesse Jones's girlfriend this year if it's the last thing I do, she vowed silently, smoothing her new denim miniskirt with restless hands. Courtney was still munching away on her sandwich, but Nicole was skipping lunch. There was no way she was going to gain back those ten pounds—especially now that the reason she'd lost them was actually around to see the results.

A sudden burst of loud laughter from the other side of the outdoor quad made Nicole look up, then sit bolt upright on her concrete bench. A group of varsity football players had just wandered onto the large paved square. Nicole strained to see if Jesse's familiar figure was among the others, and a moment later her efforts were rewarded.

There he is! she thought, her heart pounding

double-time. The sudden rush of blood in combination with her totally empty stomach made her feel lightheaded. Nicole inched forward to the edge of the bench, willing Jesse to look her way with all her mental powers, but nothing happened. She sighed impatiently. If only they had a class together this year! Instead, she was halfway through the second day of school and she still hadn't even said hello.

"I'm going to talk to him," she muttered, rising uncertainly to her feet. "There's no reason I can't say hi."

"Say hi to who?" Courtney asked. Nicole had completely forgotten that her friend was still sitting right next to her.

"Oh, uh, just someone I know from English last year. Back in a minute," she said hastily.

But Courtney was too smart for her. "A *guy* you know from English?" she asked, the corners of her eyes crinkling with amusement.

"No . . . well . . . yes. It's—it's just a guy, all right? I'll be right back." Nicole hurried off across the concrete, Courtney's laughter pelting her in the back.

I don't care if she knows, Nicole told herself as she walked. *It's only Court, and if Jesse and I get together she's going to find out anyway.* Nicole tossed her head resolutely, trusting her shoulder-length blond hair to fall into place. Her hair and her eyes were the only two features Nicole felt she could count on. Her hair was always cut in the latest style, and most people looked twice when they saw her eyes the first time—big, wide, and so blue they were almost turquoise.

Seconds later, she reached Jesse's group. Widening her eyes for maximum effect, Nicole licked her lipstick and took the plunge.

"Hi, Jesse."

Jesse was laughing at something one of the other players had said. He stopped at the sound of his name and turned in her direction. "What? Oh. Hi, Nicole."

"Hi," she repeated, thrilled. He remembered her! "How was your summer?"

"My summer?" He shrugged. "My summer was hot as hell. I don't know how you people stand living here."

Nicole smiled nervously. "We're used to it, I guess. Is it a lot cooler in California?"

"It is at the beach." Jesse's gaze wandered away from hers. He was already losing interest.

"You don't care about the weather," she teased, desperate to regain his attention. "You just miss all those *Baywatch* types in their bikinis."

Her strategy worked—a slow smile lit Jesse's face. "I can think of a few people around here I wouldn't mind seeing in a bikini." His eyes skimmed purposefully up and down her body, lingering on her bare legs.

Nicole blushed at the unexpected compliment,

but she didn't back down. "You never know," she said mysteriously. "Certain things can be arranged."

A couple of his football friends snickered, but Jesse's smile grew even wider and more flirtatious. "Really? Where exactly would a guy sign up for something like that?"

Nicole tried to match his suggestive smile, but inside she was in a state of total mental panic. She was already in way over her head in the flirting department, and now she couldn't think of a clever comeback. Her palms began to sweat, and the back of her neck burned as if stung by a bee. Meanwhile, Jesse was watching her . . . waiting. For a second she thought she might actually throw up. If she blew this chance . . .

"Ah, man. There goes Melanie Andrews," Gary Baldwin broke in, a slight sigh in his voice. "Do you think she knows how it affects us guys when she walks that way?"

"She always walks that way," Barry Stein pointed out.

"Exactly. That's my point." Gary strained to keep Melanie in view as she wove through the crowd in the quad.

Jesse's gaze dropped Nicole like a football he was about to kick, his eyes searching the quad for Melanie. When he found her, they widened appreciatively. "That's quite a dress," was all he said. It was all he *needed* to say.

Reluctantly, Nicole turned to look, her own moment with Jesse gone beyond recall. Today CCHS's cheerleading phenomenon was wearing a strappy, slinky sundress, her famous butterscotch-blond hair falling loosely to her bare shoulders. Melanie was short—probably five-foot-four—but it was impossible to think of her as anything other than "petite." The shortness of her flowered sundress and the long expanse of tan, shapely leg between its hem and the soles of her platform clogs made her seem as tall and lean as any model.

Envy turned Nicole's breathing shallow. Of *course* Jesse was looking at Melanie. What sane guy wouldn't be? Between her perfect body, flawless tan, and gorgeous hair, there wasn't a lot to find fault with. If only Nicole had made the cheering squad, then maybe she'd have *something* to compete with. But no, Melanie had beat her there, too.

"Hey, I'll see you around, Nicole. Okay?" Jesse said suddenly. "I just remembered I need to tell Melanie something."

Before Nicole could reply, he was off, abandoning her to his football friends. She stood paralyzed at the edge of their group while they joked and jeered and wished they were Jesse. Thankfully, the end-of-lunch bell rang a second later, sparing her the humiliation of listening to any more of their wisecracks.

Nicole spun on her heel and pushed hastily toward the main building, her eyes brimming with tears. She didn't even walk back past the bench where she'd left Courtney. All she could think about was getting away, being alone. She ducked inside the main building and melted gratefully into the hallway traffic, invisible at last.

"It doesn't have to be a big deal," Leah Rosenthal replied calmly, rising from her seat to more easily address her biology teacher. "I just wondered if you've ever read *On the Origin of Species*."

"And I don't see what that has to do with anything." But under the snap in Ms. Walker's voice there was a clear note of nervousness.

"It has *everything* to do with it. *On the Origin of Species* is the seminal work on evolution. Of course, Darwin did borrow like crazy from Lyell. You've read Lyell, right? *Principles of Geology?*"

"Leah, please take your seat."

An excited murmur ran through the classroom— the other students were apparently starting to find the exchange pretty fascinating.

"Tell me you've at least read Chambers's *Vestiges of Creation*. That one's short."

"I said, sit down, Leah."

Leah shook her head in disbelief. This woman was proposing to teach her evolution, and so far it looked as if Leah knew more about the subject than her teacher. Ms. Walker was young and fresh out of college, so Leah wasn't expecting miracles, but still . . . how could she even call herself a biologist if she hadn't read Darwin? Meanwhile, the murmur in the classroom was growing into a rumble.

"It just seems to me that with evolution being such a loaded subject, you ought to know it upside down before you try to teach it."

"What do you mean loaded?" Ms. Walker asked. "Evolution's been proven beyond a shadow of a doubt."

Leah smiled. "Tell that to the creationists."

The simmering class erupted into a boil—their delighted shouts and laughter echoed off the walls. Ms. Walker blushed furiously and Leah worried that perhaps she'd gone too far. On the other hand, these were all important questions. "I mean, you've read the Bible, right?" Leah added. "At least Genesis."

Ms. Walker made one last futile attempt to put the matter to rest. "Of course I haven't read *all* of the material you've mentioned, Leah. You're talking about thousands of pages. But I can assure you I've read some very competent summaries."

"If you haven't read the originals, how would you know a good summary from a bad one?" There were more howls of laughter, but Leah kept on doggedly. "Don't you think you ought to get your information from the source before you make up your mind about it?"

"*No one* reads all that stuff," the teacher protested, exasperated. "Now, sit *down*, Leah!"

Leah shrugged. "I've read it. Cover to cover." Then, reluctantly, she took her seat. As she did, she noticed a cute, dark-haired guy a couple of seats forward and to her left watching her with interest. Leah nodded, then averted her eyes, unwilling to smile in case it gave the impression that she was in the *habit* of making trouble. She wasn't. The truth was that she was at least as upset by the whole scene as Ms. Walker was. Debating evolution with someone who knew what she was talking about could have been a great experience, but now Leah knew it wasn't going to happen. Maybe having college professors for parents had spoiled her. It had certainly taught her to consider her sources.

At last the hubbub died down enough for the teacher to continue her drab lecture. Leah listened with one ear, avoiding eye contact with her curious fellow students by pretending she needed to take notes. After fifteen minutes that felt like years, the bell finally sounded.

Most of the students surged to their feet. Leah looked up to see that dark-haired guy standing by his desk, checking her out again. She smiled slightly and he smiled back. Then he stuffed his book into his backpack and headed out the door.

After he was gone, Leah turned to a girl lagging behind in the row next to hers.

"Did you see that guy?" Leah asked. "The cute one who just left?"

"Uh, *yeah*. Who didn't?" The girl's surprised expression seemed to say she'd never heard a more stupid question.

"Do you know his name?"

Surprise turned to total amazement. "Miguel del Rios," she answered cautiously.

"Miguel del Rios," Leah repeated. "Thanks."

"You mean you really didn't *know*?" the girl asked. "Where have you been living? In a cave?"

Leah laughed. "I don't pay much attention to high-school guys."

"He's more like a high-school *god*," her classmate protested, shaking her head in disbelief. "I think you've been reading too much."

Kurt Englbehrt stood at the podium on the auditorium stage, addressing the gathering of football players and cheerleaders. "I know I'm not supposed to be here," he apologized, "but I couldn't pass up this opportunity to catch you all in one place and thank you for what you're doing for me." He looked around. "Wow," he added, temporarily distracted by the sight of so many friends. "It's really good to see you all again."

Because he was the carnival's guest of honor,

Kurt hadn't been invited to any of the planning meetings, but somehow he'd found out about this one and shown up at the end to thank his teammates. Melanie watched more than listened as Kurt spoke, unable to get past the change in his appearance since the previous June.

He doesn't look so hot, she thought. Even from a few rows away his skin appeared sallow and unhealthy, and the parts of his head that showed beneath his Wildcats baseball cap were completely bald from chemotherapy. Melanie remembered the way Kurt had looked the year before, muscular and handsome, with thick brown hair and a healthy tan, and it was hard to believe that the guy in front of her was even the same person. If she'd run into him on the street, Melanie was convinced she wouldn't have recognized him.

"I wish I could find the words to tell you all what this means to me," Kurt continued. He'd lost a scary amount of weight, but his voice was still deep and strong. "All I can say is thank you. My family thanks you, too."

"So do I," called a quiet voice from the front row.

"And Dana," Kurt added, smiling affectionately at his longtime girlfriend, Dana Fraser. Dana beamed back at him, her eyes as full of love as if he were still one of the hottest guys on campus.

"He looks like crap," Tiffany Barrett whispered loudly to Vanessa.

34

"Tiff!" Angela shushed her from a seat on the senior's other side. "Dana'll hear you!"

Tiffany rolled her eyes as if to indicate that that was the most ridiculous thing she'd ever heard. Of the eight cheerleaders on the squad, inconsiderate Tiffany was quickly becoming Melanie's least favorite. This time, however, Melanie had to admit that the girl had a point.

Kurt came down from the podium and Dana rushed to hug him. They stood off to one side of the auditorium together as the team captain, Hank Lundgreen, took the stage again.

"Okay, everyone," he said. "You all got your assignments already, so that's the end of the meeting. Don't forget about the volunteers' meeting in the cafeteria tomorrow."

Hank trotted down the stairs and walked over to talk to Kurt while everybody else rose to their feet. Melanie bided her time as the crowd cleared out, waiting for a chance to speak to Vanessa.

"Hey, Vanessa," she said casually the moment her squad leader was alone. "Have you got a minute?"

"Sure. What's up?"

"Well, it's about the carnival assignments. I don't like to complain, but I don't think it's fair to make me cook hamburgers with Jesse. I feel like maybe you're only doing it because I'm the youngest girl on the squad."

35

"So what if I am?" Vanessa said, her expression arch. "I thought you *liked* Mr. Jones."

Melanie glanced nervously around the auditorium. Luckily no one was close enough to overhear Vanessa.

"I never said I *liked* him," Melanie corrected, her soft voice low and tense. "I said I could handle him."

"Then handle him. Here's your big chance."

"Vanessa—"

"Look, Melanie, I don't know what your problem is. Somebody has to cook those burgers, and it might as well be you. It's all for a good cause, you know." Vanessa nodded across the room to where Kurt and Dana were still talking to Hank. A small, excited group had gathered around them, and Kurt's smile was enormous as he greeted each of his friends.

Melanie opened her mouth to argue, then abruptly shut it again. She knew for sure that she'd gotten stuck at the food concession because it was going to be the hottest, greasiest, least glamorous job at the entire carnival and none of the other cheerleaders wanted it. But Vanessa was right about one thing: it *was* for a good cause.

"Okay. Fine," Melanie said, giving in. Vanessa nodded smugly, and Melanie collected her things and walked slowly out of the auditorium, careful not to show how upset she was. She'd had her doubts about this carnival all along, and now it looked as if they'd been justified. It wasn't that she minded helping out—not at all. It was just . . . well . . . she wasn't sure *what* it was. It didn't seem wise to dig too deeply.

It will all be over soon enough, and then everything can go back to normal, she promised herself as she walked through the late-afternoon sunshine on her way to the bus stop. After all, flipping burgers wasn't the end of the world, and Melanie could handle a guy with a futile crush in her sleep. It would have been nicer if she hadn't had to, though. She could almost believe Jesse had wangled the entire thing on purpose.

Don't be silly, she told herself, smiling as she walked. *He isn't that smart.*

Her thoughts turned then to Jesse's recent hot pursuit of her. Jesse was good-looking—no doubt about that—not to mention athletic, popular, and extremely well off. But Melanie had seen his type a million times before. She felt as if she knew him right down to his soul. The guy was a climber. All she'd ever be to him was a way to increase the value of his own stock. Well, she still had a little more self-respect than that. She'd work with Jesse at the carnival, but if he thought things were going any further, he was in for a big surprise.

Melanie sighed, hoping they'd earn enough money at their food concession to make fending him off worthwhile. Jesse or no Jesse, she still wanted to help

Kurt. And she could *really* sympathize with what his family must be feeling. First the cancer diagnosis, then all that chemo and radiation therapy. . . . Melanie was happy to do whatever she could to make things a little easier for them. After all, she knew firsthand how terrible it was to watch someone you love . . . to see them just . . .

Sudden tears stung her eyes, and Melanie had to blink hard to keep them back. She wasn't going to think about *that* right now, not out here in the middle of campus. She put a hand to her face to shield it from anyone who might be watching.

"Hey, Melanie!" Jesse called unexpectedly from behind her. "Hey, partner! Do you need a ride home?"

With a quick, negative toss of her head, Melanie sprinted for the bus stop.

Three

"Earth to Nicole," Courtney taunted, leaving off sipping Coke through a straw. "How's the weather on Planet Jesse?"

Nicole started, then blushed brilliantly. Not a single nuance of her complete failure with Jesse the day before had been lost on Courtney, of course. Her friend had been ribbing her mercilessly for almost twenty-four hours. And now she'd just caught her staring at him across the quad. . . .

"Give me a break, could ya?" said Nicole. "It's not like *you've* never had a crush. Remember Tod Hurley in eighth grade?"

"Ah, Tod." Courtney sighed theatrically, her green eyes going fake-misty. "If he hadn't moved away, we'd probably be married by now."

"If he hadn't moved away, you'd probably be in juvie by now. You *stalked* the guy, Court."

Nicole picked a crumb of soft white bread off her sandwich and rolled it around on her tongue. She was starving, but there was no way she was going to eat the lunch her mother had packed for her.

Puffing up like a lump of yeast dough wouldn't solve her problems.

"It's not stalking if you're in love," Courtney declared.

"Yeah? That's not what the victims say."

Courtney laughed good-humoredly. "All right, so I had a little crush in the eighth grade. What's that got to do with you wanting to jump Jesse Jones?"

"Courtney!" Nicole gasped.

"Oh, please. Like you've never thought about it."

"I haven't!"

"Not even a little?"

"Courtney, shut up! You're embarrassing me."

That was an understatement. Nicole could feel her cheeks heating to crimson, and she was afraid to even glance around for fear that someone had overheard them. She really loved Courtney, and she knew her friend wasn't as wild as she liked to pretend, but at moments like this Nicole wondered what they were doing together. It wasn't as if Nicole were an angel or a prude or anything, but still . . . there were limits.

"Okay, fine," Courtney said, relenting. "You just want to hold his hand. I believe you."

"Thank you." Nicole pretended not to notice the sarcasm.

Her gaze wandered gradually back to Jesse, and she chewed her bottom lip unconsciously. If only she could figure out a way to spend some time with him! Yesterday, before Melanie had made her grand appearance, he'd seemed to like her pretty well. There had to be a way she could get him alone long enough to pick up where they'd left off.

Jesse was talking to a bunch of the Wildcats. It looked like the same group as the day before, except that this time Hank Lundgreen and Kurt Englbehrt had joined them. Kurt was easy to spot in his green baseball cap with his girlfriend, Dana, at his side, her white-blond hair shining silver in the sunlight. As Nicole watched, Dana slipped her hand into Kurt's and gave it an affectionate squeeze. *It's so annoying that she gets to talk to Jesse just because she's standing there with Kurt*, Nicole thought, wishing *she* had an excuse to hang around with the football team.

And then she had an idea. "Hey, Courtney," she said excitedly. "Isn't that carnival volunteers' meeting today after school? Let's sign up to help with something."

"You've got to be kidding. I'll go to the carnival with you if you want, but I'm not spending an entire Saturday working at school for free."

"Ah, come on, Court. It's for a good cause."

Courtney snorted. "Give me a little credit. I know what cause *you're* working on."

Nicole blushed but didn't give up. "Please? It'll be fun."

"It'll be a total drag," Courtney predicted.

41

It *did* sound like kind of a drag. On the other hand, how else was she ever going to get Jesse to notice her? Nicole imagined spending another whole semester gazing at him from afar, and it wasn't a pretty picture.

She made up her mind.

If a wasted Saturday was what it took to get Jesse Jones's attention, then it was definitely worth the sacrifice.

"Don't forget to read chapter two!" Ms. Walker shouted above the din as the dismissal bell went off, signaling the end of fifth-period biology.

Leah took her time loading up her backpack, then slipped out the door at the rear of the classroom. The main hall was crowded to capacity, as always. Luckily, she didn't have far to go to her last class. She stepped out into traffic.

"Hi," said a deep male voice to her right.

Leah turned her head and smiled at the unexpected sight of Miguel del Rios walking along beside her. "Hi."

"I, uh, I'm Miguel del Rios," he said, looking slightly embarrassed. "I'm in your biology class."

"I know. My name's Leah Rosenthal."

"Yeah." Obviously he'd already done that bit of research.

There was a brief, self-conscious silence. "So, how do you like biology?" Leah asked.

The smile that lit Miguel's handsome face was spontaneous and totally real. "I'll like it fine if you keep shaking things up the way you did yesterday."

"Sorry to disappoint you. That was a big mistake."

"What do you mean? It was great!"

"Real great!" Leah laughed. "I wanted to ask the teacher a question, and I ended up starting a riot."

"Stuff happens." Miguel was still smiling.

Leah suddenly noticed he had a dimple in his chin.

The crowd buffeted them from all sides as Leah and Miguel walked side by side down the packed hallway. Leah kept close to Miguel, happy when it occurred to her that for once she didn't tower over the guy she was walking with. At her height that happened frequently, and even though those types of things weren't too important to Leah, a tall guy was a welcome change.

"So anyway, what's so exciting about evolution?" Miguel asked, his dark eyes interested.

"Only everything. The concept has all kinds of philosophical repercussions."

"And why does it matter to you?"

Leah shrugged, a half smile on her lips. "I'm really into world religions, but I won't stick my head in the sand either. I think you need to study science, too, and take it all together."

"World religions?" Miguel looked as if he couldn't believe his ears.

"Don't ask me why—religion has always fascinated me. Maybe it's because my mother is Lutheran and my father is Jewish. They both stopped practicing before they met each other, though, so I don't go to church or temple or anything. I'm not even sure what I believe. I just keep reading whatever I get my hands on. How about you?"

Leah turned to smile at Miguel but stopped short when she saw his expression. The friendliness of a moment before had vanished completely.

"I don't go to church anymore, either." His voice was flat, but not flat enough to hide his obvious irritation.

"I—I'm sorry," Leah stammered. "Did I say something?"

"It's . . . no. Whatever. I have to go to class."

Leah watched, stunned, as Miguel turned and jogged off down the hallway.

"Wow, it's crowded!" Jenna exclaimed when she and Peter stepped through the open cafeteria doors. It was surprising to see so many students staying after school voluntarily, no matter how good the reason. "Where do you want to sit?"

Peter shrugged. "You pick. Anywhere's fine with me."

Jenna wove through the long crowded tables until she found two places near the front of the room.

44

She and Peter had just taken their seats when the meeting was called to order by Hank Lundgreen.

"Okay, people, listen up!" Hank bellowed from behind a podium brought in for the occasion. The school hadn't provided a microphone, but from what Jenna had heard so far, that wasn't going to be a problem. "We've got a lot to do this afternoon, so sit down and let's get to it."

Hank paused maybe three seconds, barely long enough for anyone still left standing to drop to the floor, before resuming his address. "Okay. First, thanks for coming out today. The team's put a lot of planning into this carnival, but we wouldn't be able to pull it off without the help of the cheerleaders and the support of all of you."

A wild, spontaneous cheer sounded from the left side of the cafeteria. Jenna turned her head to see the cheerleaders gathered there, sitting with the football team.

"So, here's the deal," Hank continued. "Everything's all planned. We've already figured out all the booths and rides and ordered what we need. We're getting a free ad in the *Clearwater Herald*, and I think the local TV news is going to pick us up too. We're expecting a huge crowd, so now we need to man those booths."

There was a loud, disapproving hiss from the cheerleaders.

"*What?*" Hank protested. "Oh, come on. Woman the booths? *Person* the booths, all right?"

The cheerleaders applauded.

"*Anyway,*" Hank continued, shaking his head, "there's a player or a cheerleader or both in charge of every concession. I'm going to call the booth leaders up here one at a time to say what they're working on and how many helpers they need. If you want to volunteer for that booth, stand up. The booth leaders will pick out the people they need, then take their groups outside to discuss the details. Okay? Any questions?"

No one said anything.

"All right, then." Hank consulted a wrinkled sheet of notebook paper. "Josh Stockton."

Jenna watched as Josh swaggered up to the podium. His size was amazing for a high-school kid, and he was clearly proud of it. "I've got security," he announced importantly. "I only need a couple more guys, because we're using mostly players. *Big* guys," he corrected as boys leapt to their feet like crazy to grab that prestigious assignment.

"I guess that lets me out," Peter quipped to Jenna. He clenched his fists and tightened all the muscles in his skinny torso, as if showing off a body-builder's physique.

"You're as *tall* as he is," Jenna returned loyally.

Peter laughed. "I'm sure they're *dying* to have me on security, but I'd rather do something with you."

Josh eventually selected two imposing candidates, then herded his group out of the cafeteria.

"Barry Stein!" Hank bellowed from the podium.

Barry hurried forward to make his announcement. "I've got one of the booths selling tickets for the rides. I could use three people." Ten or so people stood up, and Barry pointed quickly to the closest three. "Come on," he told them. "Let's go out to the quad."

Hank consulted his list again. "Jesse Jones!"

A tall, brown-haired guy Jenna couldn't remember seeing before took the podium, along with Melanie Andrews, the new sophomore cheerleader.

"Melanie and I have the main food concession," Jesse announced. "We'll be cooking and serving hamburgers and hot dogs, as well as chips and lemonade. We're going to be busy all day, so we'll need six people. Any volunteers?"

Out of the corner of her eye, Jenna saw a girl with blond hair spring eagerly to her feet, her arm stretched high in the air. No one else stood up.

"Yeah, okay, Nicole. Anyone else?" The confident expression on Jesse's face eroded somewhat as he looked repeatedly back and forth across the room for additional volunteers. No one else was standing. Jenna glanced at Melanie Andrews. The popular blonde usually seemed too cool to let anything faze her, but now her exceptionally pretty face was starting to mirror the strain on Jesse's. And there was *still* nobody standing. Jenna was glad Kurt wasn't there to see such a lack of enthusiasm.

"No one else wants to volunteer because cooking hamburgers is probably the worst job they've got," she whispered to Peter. "Hot and greasy and plain hard work."

Peter nodded. "I know. Want to do it?"

At times like this Jenna remembered why Peter was her best friend. "Sure," she said with a smile.

Peter and Jenna stood up.

"Oh, good." Jesse was clearly relieved. "Come on up, you two."

They had just finished crossing to join their new group when someone else stood up. "Okay. You," Jesse called gratefully, pointing.

"I've seen that girl before," Peter whispered to Jenna as the new volunteer walked toward them. "What's her name again?"

Jenna tried to remember. The most recent addition was tall and willowy, with shoulder-length brown hair and light olive skin. She crossed the room gracefully, her head held high. "I think it's Leah," Jenna whispered back.

"Great! Thanks, Miguel," Jesse said loudly, causing Jenna's attention to whip back to the podium.

Was it possible? It *was*! She hadn't even seen him in the room, but now Miguel del Rios was coming to join them.

What incredible luck! Jenna thought, an ache in her cheeks from smiling too hard. *This must be my reward for doing the right thing!* She worked to tone down her smile into something more normal as Miguel made his way through the cafeteria, but there was nothing she could do about the pounding of her heart. It was beating as hard as if she'd just finished running the track.

"Hi," Miguel whispered to them all as he reached the growing group.

"We need one more person here," Jesse announced. "Come *on*, people, this is for Kurt."

"I'll do it!" a boy's voice piped up. "I'll join."

The group turned in unison to see its final member—a nerdy-looking kid with straight blond hair parted down the middle and thick horn-rimmed glasses. He looked at least two years younger than any of the rest of them and he stumbled clumsily as he made his way through the tables, tripping repeatedly over feet, books, and backpacks.

"Oh, perfect," Jenna heard the girl named Nicole mutter under her breath. "It's Screech from *Saved by the Bell*."

"Screech is taller," Miguel whispered back.

The girl smiled appreciatively. "And a snappier dresser."

49

"Hi!" the kid said when he finally reached their group. He thrust his right hand out in front of him, a shy, embarrassed smile on his face. "I'm Ben Pipkin."

Everyone froze and stared in horror—everyone but Peter. "Hi, Ben," he said, stepping forward to shake Ben's hand. "I'm Peter. And this is my best friend, Jenna."

"Leah Rosenthal," the tall girl said, stepping forward to shake as well.

"Miguel del Rios." Miguel didn't shake.

They all turned expectantly to the blonde. "Nicole Brewster," she said automatically, barely looking at them. Her almost unnaturally blue eyes were fixed instead on Jesse and Melanie, who were just walking over to the group.

"Okay, everyone. Thanks for helping," Jesse said. The way he looked Ben over while he said it seemed to imply he wasn't any too sure about his final volunteer.

Jenna felt a stab of sympathy for Ben. He hadn't even said anything yet, and half the group was already against him. Ben wasn't the coolest guy Jenna had ever seen—and he certainly wasn't the smoothest—but he still deserved a chance. Jenna decided to be extra nice to him, to compensate for the others.

"Let's go outside," Melanie suggested. "There's a good spot behind the cafeteria."

"Right," said Jesse. "Come on, everyone. We'll take the side door."

The group of eight strung out into single file as Melanie led the way to the door, Peter and Jenna at the rear. They were almost there when Ben tripped over his own sneaker. His arms flew out frantically to stop his fall, sending his books into a noisy, flapping orbit. Still off balance, he careened heavily into Miguel, who somehow managed to stay on his feet and at the same time grab the smaller guy by one skinny biceps. Ben dangled heavily from Miguel's one-handed grip, his worn sneakers scrabbling frantically to regain their footing on the slick linoleum. The students in the cafeteria howled with spontaneous, raucous laughter, and Jenna winced as she realized that everyone there was watching. Miguel finally grabbed Ben by the other arm as well and hauled him back onto his feet.

"Thanks," Ben murmured, clearly mortified. He stood blushing for a second, then dove to retrieve his books, smacking skulls with Leah, who had already bent to pick them up. Leah fell backward from the impact, both hands clasping her injured head. A fresh wave of laughter swept the cafeteria.

"Oops," Ben said, his cheeks turning an even more intense shade of red. "Sorry, Leah." He tried to take her hand to help her up, but Leah waved him off, standing on her own.

The poor guy, Jenna thought. She could feel her own cheeks flushing as the mocking laughter went on and on.

Peter leaned over to whisper in her ear. "Let's be nice to Ben," he said. "That poor kid's going to need all the help he can get."

Four

"Nicole! Mom said it's your turn to vacuum!" Nicole's younger sister, Heather, cried triumphantly the second Nicole got home from school on Thursday.

"So what, Heathen." Nicole breezed past her sibling on her way upstairs to her room.

"You'd better stop calling me that or I'll tell Mom when she gets back from the grocery store," Heather whined, following along behind her. "It's not true, and it's not nice!"

"That's the idea," Nicole muttered under her breath. She reached her bedroom and walked inside, tossing her backpack onto her desk.

"I'll tell Greg," Heather threatened, reappearing in her doorway. "He'll tell Pastor Ramsey and then you *will* be in trouble."

Greg was Heather's new Sunday-school teacher, and Nicole was pretty sure her sister thought *he* was the one who'd walked on water. All she ever talked about was Greg—Greg said this, Greg did that. . . .

"Will you get out of here? You've got Sunday

school on the brain." Nicole pushed her sister backward out into the hall and shut the door in her face.

"You—you'd better vacuum the carpet!" Heather sputtered furiously from the other side.

"Yeah, yeah," Nicole muttered, crossing her room to close the bathroom door as well. The way the house was built, her room and Heather's had a bathroom between them with a door on either side. The last thing Nicole needed was that stringy-haired little pest coming around to bug her through their bathroom. The way she felt today, if Heather barged into her room it could be her sister's final act on Earth.

Because Nicole was in a terrible mood. The first week of school was almost over, and so far things couldn't have gone worse. Jesse still didn't know she was alive, Courtney was giving her nothing but grief about that stupid dating bet, and yesterday she'd gained half a pound! And that was just for starters—volunteering to help out with that ridiculous carnival had been the biggest mistake of her life. She wished she'd never come up with such a featherbrained idea!

Nicole stripped off her school dress and threw it disgustedly over the back of her desk chair. She'd worn a brand-new outfit every day for the last four days, and she *still* might as well have been invisible. What was wrong with her? Why didn't anyone notice? Why didn't *Jesse* notice?

Depressed, she grabbed the latest issue of *Modern Girl* from her nightstand and plopped down onto the bed to read it, hoping to take her mind off her problems. But that afternoon the photos didn't hold her attention the way they usually did, and the words in the articles blurred and ran together. Nicole flipped idly through the pages, trying to concentrate, but she couldn't. Her mind kept going back to that horrible carnival meeting she'd attended the day before.

Once that geek Ben had finished embarrassing them all in front of the entire cafeteria, her group had finally gone outside to "plan" things. As it turned out, planning things consisted mostly of Jesse telling everyone what to do while making cow eyes at Melanie Andrews. It made Nicole's stomach revolt to remember the way he'd kept gazing at Melanie, consulting her on every little detail.

As if on cue, her stomach growled indignantly, interrupting Nicole's train of thought. She hadn't eaten a single bite all day—after the half pound she'd gained yesterday, she wasn't taking any chances—but now it was nearly four o'clock and she was starving. She felt her hipbones through the slick fabric of her slip, gauging how far they protruded above her stomach. They seemed sharper than they had that morning, so hopefully all her suffering was paying off.

She snuggled down deeper into the softness of

her bedspread and began paying more attention to the magazine photographs. Soon her mom would be back from the store, and then her father would get home from work. When that happened Nicole would have to go down to dinner and put up with Heather and vacuum the house and do whatever else they all dreamed up for her. But for the next hour or two, while she could, Nicole wasn't going to do anything but relax and look at her magazines. After the week she'd had, she'd earned it.

Nicole turned a page and was confronted by an article titled *Are You and Your Man Compatible? Ten Sure Ways to Find Out.* Her heart raced excitedly at the mere thought of learning something so important. Were she and Jesse compatible? Even if they weren't, did it matter? Jesse was so handsome, Nicole felt as if she could spend the rest of her life just looking at him. She closed her eyes and called up his face in her memory—the veiled blue eyes, the straight, chiseled nose, those completely kissable lips.

The article turned out to be several pages longer than Nicole had expected and, even though she spent an hour studying every word, in the end it didn't shed much light on her situation with Jesse. *Oh well,* she thought, flipping the page.

The next major feature was a quiz called *Rate Your Sex Appeal.* Nicole hurried to her desk and rummaged eagerly for a pen. She was only halfway through the questions, though, when Mrs. Brewster's voice rang out from downstairs.

"Nicole! Dinner!"

Already? Nicole bolted up off her bed and checked the clock on her nightstand. It was nearly five-thirty. "Great," she grumbled, dropping the magazine onto the floor.

"Coming!" she yelled to her mother. She hurriedly pulled her slip off over her head, then crossed to her dresser for some clothes. On the way there, though, her attention was arrested by the sight of her nearly naked body in the full-length mirror on the back of her bathroom door. She paused, gazing at her image. *If only I were thinner!* she thought. *Like those models in the magazines.* Then *maybe I could get Jesse Jones to look my way. . . .*

"*Nicole!*" her mother called again, sounding annoyed.

"Coming, Mom!" Tearing herself away from the mirror, Nicole hurriedly pulled on a pair of jeans and a CCHS sweatshirt, then burst out of her room and galloped down the stairs, taking them two at a time.

Her parents and sister were already seated around the dining room table. "There you are!" said Mrs. Brewster. "It's about time."

"Sorry." Nicole pulled out a chair and joined her family. They bowed their heads. "For what we are about to receive, may the Lord make us truly thankful. Amen."

"Amen."

"Nicole, pass the potatoes to your father," her mother said without missing a beat. "Heather, you put some of those peas on your plate, young lady."

"*Mom . . .*"

"Do it."

The next few minutes were spent passing plates and serving food. Ever since Nicole had started dieting, she'd come to dread this part of the day more than any other. It was easy to get away with skipping breakfast and lunch, but eating dinner under her parents' noses meant she had to be more careful. She took a heaping spoonful of peas and a lot of salad without dressing. That made her plate look full enough to get away with essentially no potatoes and a single chicken wing.

"How was work today, dear?" her mother asked her father.

Mr. Brewster grunted noncommittally. "The same."

Nicole looked across the table to where her father absentmindedly chewed a drumstick. He was getting older, she realized. His once brown hair was thinning and turning silver. The brown eyes behind his glasses looked bloodshot and exhausted, and permanent dark circles had etched themselves beneath them.

Her mother, on the other hand, still looked like a homecoming queen. Mrs. Brewster's blond hair was done in an elaborate, Ivana Trump-style puff, and the sleeveless pink sheath she wore was silk. It clung to her ultraslim figure just right. Her eyeliner was heavy, to emphasize the astonishing blue of the eyes Nicole had inherited, but the rest of her makeup was tasteful. And then there were the accessories. Mrs. Brewster was big on accessories. Tonight she had on silver button earrings, a silver chain belt, and strappy silver sandals. Next to her mother, Nicole always felt half finished, like a project someone had given up on when they'd realized how it was going to turn out.

"Can we get to church early this week?" Heather wanted to know. "Greg said whoever got there first could help him set up something special for the class."

"How early?" Mrs. Brewster asked warily.

"I don't know. An hour?"

"Oh, Heather. Not an hour. What would the rest of us do there so early?"

"Beats me," Heather admitted. "Maybe you could go into the church and pray."

"For an hour? I don't think so."

Nicole tuned out the conversation the second it became clear she was in no danger of being sucked into Heather's stupid plan. The Brewsters went to church every Sunday, but sometimes Nicole wondered why. Her little sister was the only one who seemed to get anything out of it. Nicole believed in God, of course, but he wasn't something she needed to think about every minute. Or even every Sunday, for that matter. The Sunday-school discussion dragged on as Nicole's thoughts turned to Jesse.

Maybe she was giving up before she was beaten on this carnival thing. It still gave her a royal pain in the rear that Melanie Andrews, Miss Perfect, had to be in her group, but now that Nicole was thinking about it, Melanie hadn't seemed nearly as interested in Jesse as he had in her. The sudden realization excited her. *Maybe there's hope after all*, Nicole thought. In any event, there was no point in throwing in the towel now, not when she still had an entire day with Jesse to look forward to.

Who knew? If Nicole played her cards right on Saturday, maybe she *would* have something to thank God for in church this Sunday.

Leah flopped restlessly onto her side and checked the time on the glowing digital clock beside her bed: twelve-thirty and she *still* couldn't fall asleep. At this rate, tomorrow she was going to feel as if someone had put her through the spin cycle and hung her out to dry.

She rolled onto her back and sighed, annoyed.

Leah wasn't used to losing sleep. Not for any reason, and *certainly* not for a guy. If she hadn't already been irritated with Miguel, this would have clinched it for sure.

What was his story, anyway? The way he'd acted in the hall after biology on Wednesday had been bizarre. Then, an hour later, he'd shown up at the carnival meeting and signed up for the same team she did! Leah was willing to take that as an apology, but when she'd tried to talk to him after the meeting, he'd been cold and standoffish.

"Sorry about that thing in the hall," he'd muttered, not meeting her eyes. "I don't really like to talk about stuff like that."

"Like what?"

"Religion and stuff. You know."

"What *do* you like to talk about?"

He'd smiled wanly. "I don't much like to talk."

Whatever. It wasn't as if it mattered to Leah one way or the other. She wasn't looking for anything from Miguel. It just bugged her the way he'd started something with her and then backed off for no reason. Today, after biology, he'd taken off running the second the bell rang, as if he were terrified she might try to speak to him again.

And that's why I never waste my time with high-school boys, Leah reminded herself, flipping all the way over in her hot, tangled sheets *They aren't nearly worth the trouble.*

61

On Friday afternoon, Melanie hurried from her sixth-period class to the grassy area behind the cafeteria. *Jesse had better make this quick*, she thought.

As far as Melanie was concerned, they'd settled everything on Wednesday, but Jesse had taken it into his head at lunchtime to hold one last group meeting before the carnival. The two of them had spent their entire lunch period just trying to find the other six people. It was a miracle that they'd succeeded at all, especially with Ben, who apparently thought it was cool to eat by himself on the soccer field.

"Melanie! There you are!" Jesse called too loudly as she rounded the corner of the cafeteria. "Everyone's here, then."

"Hi." Melanie smiled and nodded at the others. *Hurry up, Jesse*, she thought. *I have to catch the bus*.

"I just wanted to have this one last meeting," Jesse explained, "because I had a great idea. I think we should all dress up Hawaiian-style tomorrow."

"You called a meeting for *that?*" Melanie blurted out before she could stop herself. "I'm going to miss my bus for *that?*"

"No problem," said Jesse. "I'll give you a ride."

Yeah, no problem for you, Melanie thought, folding her arms and glaring at him. *That was probably part of your plan all along!*

"I don't mind dressing up if everyone else wants to," Jenna said tentatively.

Melanie glanced at her. *She has perfect skin*, she thought, temporarily distracted. *She ought to wear some makeup.* What Jenna *was* wearing, Melanie noticed, was a large gold cross.

"I could go either way," said Leah.

"Me too," said Peter.

"Well, *I* think it's a great idea," Nicole put in enthusiastically. "It will make our booth stand out from everyone else's. What do you think we should wear, Jesse?"

"I don't know. Maybe the guys could wear Hawaiian shirts and shorts, and maybe you girls could get hold of some hula skirts or something. You know, the grass kind."

"Oh, there it is," Melanie said bitingly, her patience finally exhausted. "With coconut halves on top, I suppose. You'd like that, wouldn't you, Jesse?"

The rest of the group turned to stare at her as if she'd suddenly lost her mind. Even Jesse managed to look amazed.

"I wasn't thinking anything like that, Melanie, I swear. I only wanted our group to be the best—so we could earn the most money for Kurt. I thought if we had a theme, with costumes and decorations and everything, it might attract more customers."

He sounded so sincere that Melanie almost regretted her accusation. "All the money's going to the same place," she said in a humbler tone. "It doesn't matter who makes the most."

"You're right," Jesse agreed. "I'm just competitive, I guess. But after all, if a thing's worth doing, it's worth kicking butt at, right?"

"I really don't think it matters what we wear," Miguel del Rios broke in. "Let's just agree to the Hawaiian idea, and everyone can do it however they want."

"I can borrow my dad's Hawaiian shirt," Ben said excitedly. "He and my mom went to Oahu for their anniversary, and he got this really cool one with pineapples and—"

"That's good, Ben," Jesse interrupted. Melanie looked over in time to catch the slight roll of his eyes. "You wear that. Now, who wants to meet me here early to set up the tarps and grills?"

"I do!" Ben volunteered immediately.

"Um, okay. I could really use more help, though." Jesse glanced at Miguel, who remained silent. "Peter, could you come too?"

"Sure thing," said Peter, smiling. When he smiled, he was almost handsome, Melanie realized to her surprise. He was so tall and skinny and quiet that she hadn't noticed before.

"Melanie?" Jesse turned in her direction.

"Don't look at me! We girls are already meeting at the crack of dawn to squeeze those stupid lemons, remember?" *Fresh* lemonade had been another of Jesse's brilliant ideas.

"Oh, yeah. Well, Peter and Ben and I can probably handle it. What do you guys think about decorating the booth? Maybe we could have some streamers or a sign or something."

"I know it's not very exciting, but we ought to have a menu showing all the prices," Leah said. "I can make that, if you want."

"Good idea," said Nicole. "And we've got lots of leftover party decorations at my house. Do you want me to look through them to see what we can use?"

"Sure." Jesse flashed her a smile.

"How about a sign for our booth?" Jenna suggested. "We could give ourselves a funny name or something."

"Oh! Oh! I know!" Ben said excitedly. "What about Team Take-out?"

Most of the group members chuckled and Melanie's eyebrows shot up with surprise. Who'd have guessed that nerdy Ben actually had a sense of humor? "That's kind of cute," she said.

"Okay, team, that's settled then," Jesse said in a raspy, unnatural voice. He put both hands to his head, smoothing his hair straight back, and Melanie suddenly realized he was attempting to imitate Coach Davis. She felt sorry for the people who didn't know what was coming next.

Jesse paced distractedly a few seconds, then wheeled back on the group, screaming at the top of his lungs. "Everyone has their assignments, and now I expect this team to get fired *up*!" he bellowed, scaring Ben nearly out of his saddle shoes. "Tomorrow, when they count up the bucks at the end of the day, I want this whole school to know that *Team Take-out rules*!"

Five

"You look ridiculous," Heather said with a smirk, sticking her head through the doorway on her side of the bathroom. "What are you supposed to be, anyway? A hula-school dropout?"

"Get *out* of here, Heathen!" Nicole shrieked, pushing her sister out of the bathroom and slamming the door behind her. "Mind your own business!"

"All right, but you look stupid," Heather insisted, her voice carrying through the door. "Everyone's going to laugh at you."

"They are not!"

But now the little pain in the butt had her worried. Nicole ran back into her bedroom to check her reflection in the full-length mirror. She was wearing her cutest flowered bikini, over which she'd tied on a somewhat threadbare grass skirt she'd found in the party junk in the basement. Bright pink and yellow plastic leis around her neck and wrists completed her ensemble. She wished she were thinner, of course, but even so she thought her outfit looked pretty good.

She decided to ignore Heather's comment and turned to dig though her closet for some old khaki sneakers that more or less blended in. Then she picked up her backpack full of decorations and headed down the stairs. "Mom, Dad, I'm leaving!" she called.

Mrs. Brewster wandered out of the kitchen and did a horrified double take. "Not dressed like that, you aren't. Go put on some clothes."

"Mom! *Everyone's* dressing like this. We're wearing Hawaiian costumes."

"Well, *your* costume is going to include some shorts, at the very least," Mrs. Brewster said firmly. "Really, Nicole. Half the town's coming to this thing, and I can see right through that skirt."

"I'm *wearing* bathing suit bottoms," Nicole whined.

"Shorts," Mrs. Brewster repeated. "I'm not kidding."

Tears sprang to Nicole's eyes at the unfairness of it all. Hadn't Jesse said he wouldn't mind seeing her in a bikini? And then he'd given her this custom-made excuse to wear one. Next to Melanie, Nicole was going to look like an inconspicuous little goody-goody in shorts! Meanwhile, her mother was blocking the front door, her hands on her hips.

"Fine," Nicole said petulantly, running back up the stairs. But as she dug through her dresser, a sly smile crept onto her face.

She'd put on some shorts to get past her mom, but there was nothing to stop her from taking them off again at school.

Leah strode across the dew-damp grass on her way to the gym, enjoying the cool morning air. It was a beautiful day for a carnival and sure to be hot later on. *It's a good thing we're serving lemonade!* she thought, knowing they'd probably drink plenty of it themselves.

A figure crossing the lawn from the opposite direction waved, and Leah recognized Jenna. She waved back, then stopped to wait.

"Hi! Are you ready to do this?" Jenna asked, her blue eyes sparkling. "Are those the signs?" she added excitedly before Leah could answer the first question.

"Yeah. What do you think?" Leah held the two poster-sized cardboard signs up for inspection. One carefully lettered, no-nonsense board spelled out the menu items and prices in black block letters, but on the other Leah had let her imagination go wild. Team Take-out! the sign proclaimed in shocking pink script. The edge of the sign featured a border of swaying palm trees with hula-dancing hamburgers and hot dogs.

"Oh, cool!" Jenna exclaimed, reaching out to touch it. "You're an artist!"

Leah laughed, embarrassed. "Not really. I don't know what came over me."

"Well, whatever it was, I'm glad it did. Do you want me to carry one?" Jenna was wearing a backpack, but she held out her hands to show they were empty.

"Nah, they're light." The two girls resumed walking to the gym.

"I'm glad you wore pants," Jenna confided in a relieved voice. "There was no way I was showing up in public in a grass skirt."

Leah smiled. "I'll be amazed if anyone does. Jesse was just throwing out ideas."

"Well, anyway, I'm glad," Jenna repeated, glancing down at her Hawaiian shirt and chinos. "This is a lot less embarrassing. By the way, your top is cute."

"Thanks." Leah had decided on a hibiscus-print halter top and white shorts. "I hope my shorts don't get too dirty."

Jenna shrugged. "They probably will, but who cares? It's for a good cause. I'm glad we can do this for Kurt."

"Do you know him?" Leah asked.

"Not really. Peter and I don't hang out with the football crowd too often. How about you?"

"I probably hang out with athletes even less than you do, but I still wanted to help. It seemed like the right thing to do, you know?"

"Absolutely," said Jenna, beaming. "I'm glad we ended up on the same team."

"Yeah. Me too."

And she *was* happy to be working with Jenna, Leah realized. Miguel, on the other hand . . . well, that depended on whether he was Jekyll or Hyde today.

"Okay!" Melanie straightened up and wiped her juice-covered hands with a sodden, disintegrating paper towel. The sharp, sweet smell of freshly squeezed lemons filled the air, competing with the normal gymnasium odors of sweat, chlorine, and Pine Sol. "How many is that?"

Jenna checked the boxes behind her. "That was the third case. Only two more to go."

"Really? Wow!" Melanie exclaimed. "This is going faster than I thought it would. Maybe Jesse isn't such a dimwit after all."

Jenna and Leah laughed and kept working at the large folding table assigned to their group. Leah had devised a system: she sliced each lemon in two, then passed half to Melanie and half to Jenna, who squeezed them using large, restaurant-style presses.

"No, I mean it," Melanie said. "This could have been a lot worse. I really appreciate you guys coming out early to help me."

"We *wanted* to help," Jenna said, reaching for another lemon.

71

"Yeah, no problem," Leah said. "But I wonder why Nicole didn't show."

"I don't know." Melanie glanced toward the open doorway. There were a few other groups working in the gym, and assorted people hurried back and forth in a frantic rush of last-minute preparations, but there was no sign of Nicole. "I thought she was going to be here."

She'd no sooner said it than Nicole rushed through the nearest side door wearing a tiny bikini and a scraggly fake grass skirt. "Am I very late?" she asked, hurrying over with strands of green plastic trailing out behind her.

"Not very," Melanie answered, stunned. Was Nicole actually planning to cook hamburgers dressed like that?

Nicole seemed equally surprised as she looked from Melanie to Jenna to Leah. "Am I the only one wearing a grass skirt? I thought we were all going to!"

Melanie shook her head. "In Jesse's twisted dreams. He's lucky I humored him this far. I still might change into pants." For now, Melanie was wearing a Hawaiian-print dress with hot pink shorts underneath—in case she had to bend over.

Nicole finally seemed to realize the magnitude of her mistake. She glanced down at her skimpy outfit, then nervously back at Melanie. "I, uh, have some shorts in the car. Maybe I'll run and put them on. I . . . um . . . don't want to get too sunburned."

Nicole's pale cheeks had already turned pink—with embarrassment.

"I brought an extra shirt if you want to wear it," Jenna offered. "It would keep the sun off your shoulders." She wiped her hands on a towel, then pulled a cute, short-sleeved Hawaiian shirt out of her backpack. "I thought we might need it if someone got spilled on, but you take it, Nicole."

"Really? Thanks." Nicole reached for the shirt eagerly. "I—I'm just going to run back to my car and change, and then I promise I'll help you guys."

"No hurry," Leah said, slicing another lemon and handing both pieces to Jenna. "We're practically done, anyway."

"At this rate, we'll be able to get out to the football field early and help the guys," Jenna added.

"I'll be right back," Nicole promised, running out the door with the extra shirt clutched in her hand.

"You just saved that girl's life. You know that, right?" Leah told Jenna.

"No kidding!" Melanie agreed. A bikini at a carnival was a fashion "don't" even she would never have lived down. "What you just did practically qualifies as an act of mercy."

Jenna shrugged, her creamy skin flushing. "It's only a shirt."

***

Jenna stood back and surveyed their finished concession stand. "It's perfect!" she proclaimed. "Wow, you guys, it looks great."

"Not bad, if I do say so," Jesse said proudly.

The four guys had rigged an elaborate structure of tables, steel poles, and blue plastic tarps that not only defined the limits of the booth, but also provided some shade for the workers. Leah's menu and the TEAM TAKE-OUT! sign had been hung up high for everyone to see, and the entire group had gone wild taping on the streamers and puffed-paper pineapples Nicole had brought from home. Colorful twists of paper fluttered in every hint of a breeze, and smoke from the two enormous barbecue grills spiraled lazily upward. Under the tables, coolers held iced-down hamburgers and hot dogs, while buns and potato chips stood at the ready in neatly stacked cardboard boxes. Another two coolers were stuffed with block and crushed ice for the lemonade.

As Jenna watched, Leah finished screwing the pump onto a big plastic jar of ketchup and set it down next to a similar one of mustard. In divided steel compartments next to the pumps were lettuce and tomato slices, chopped onions, relish, pickle chips, and mayonnaise in plastic packets—all provided courtesy of the school cafeteria.

"We're ready," Jesse said loudly. "All we need now is our first customer."

"We're not *that* ready," Melanie told him. She

was squatting on the grass next to an industrial-sized plastic drink container, a jug of sugar syrup in her hand. "How much sugar do I put in the lemonade?"

"A lot," said Leah, hurrying to help her.

Ben wandered over to watch, and Jenna had to work to suppress a giggle at the sight of him. The other guys looked cute in their Hawaiian shirts and shorts. But Ben! He hadn't been kidding when he'd said he was going to borrow his father's shirt—the gaudy rayon print shirt was so enormous it looked as if he was playing dress-up. It hung and billowed and drooped, and there was so much extra fabric tucked in that it stuck out below the hem of his shorts and tickled his bony white legs. Jenna forced herself to look away, and accidentally locked eyes with Peter.

"Want to take a quick tour of the rest of the carnival?" he asked, smiling to let her know he'd caught her checking Ben's fashion statement. "They're going to open the gates in a minute."

"I wish we could!" Jenna answered, looking down the field. Booths crowded both sides of the football stadium—from where she stood she could see games, crafts, baked goods, T-shirts, a burst of multicolored helium balloons, and a whirring cotton-candy machine. The various tarps, table-cloths, and items for sale all blurred into a bright, haphazard patchwork.

"Miguel said they were setting up rides in the parking lot when he drove in," Peter told her.

"Well, we'll get a break sometime. We can look around then."

"Why not now? We're ready to go, and we could be back before they open."

Jenna had to admit, Peter's plan was tempting.

"Hey, Jesse!" Peter yelled. "Jenna and I are going to look around. Back in ten minutes."

Jesse grunted some sort of affirmative answer. He and Miguel were busy pouring two five-gallon bottles of drinking water into the lemonade container. Smiling, Peter grabbed Jenna's hand and dragged her off to cruise the carnival.

Team Take-out's setup was near the entrance, so people would be sure to see it, but they by no means had the monopoly on food. There were candy apples, peanuts, popcorn, caramel corn, ice cream, baked goods, Sno-Kones, and even big, gooey cinnamon rolls from a bakery in town. Jenna and Peter raced along, taking it all in. At one end of the gymnasium parking lot was a fun zone, with rides and games for prizes.

"Look, a Ferris wheel," said Peter. He knew that was her favorite.

Jenna nodded, hoping they'd get a chance to ride it. "We'd better go back now."

They rushed back to their station, where the sight that met their eyes made it obvious they hadn't returned a second too soon. Jesse, Miguel, Ben, and Leah were trying to lift the now-full lemonade container off the grass onto the serving table. The huge vat was obviously enormously heavy, and the foursome didn't seem to have a very good grip on it.

"Uh-oh," Peter said. "I don't think they should have filled that up on the ground." He rushed forward to help just as Ben lost his grip on the slippery plastic. The giant vat lurched wildly and Ben stumbled forward at the sudden release of weight. A rogue wave of lemonade crested over the top of the open container, smacking him right in the face.

"Be careful! Don't drop it!" Melanie cried.

Luckily, Peter managed to grab Ben's side of the vat. More lemonade slopped out, drenching the front of Peter's shirt and splashing crazily in all directions, but the group eventually got the container back under control and set it down on a table at the front of the booth. A puddle spread out immediately, soaking the white paper tablecloth.

"What a mess," Miguel said, looking around for something to wipe his hands on. He settled for his shorts.

"You're not kidding." Peter pulled the soaked front of his shirt away from his chest and vainly tried to shake it dry.

"Now I'm all sticky," Leah complained.

Then everyone looked at Ben. His enormous shirt was plastered to his underdeveloped frame, his hair was drenched and dripping, and the thick lenses of his glasses were steaming up from the moisture. As Jenna watched, he snatched them off his face and wiped them on his wet shirt, making things even worse. "At least now we have room to add the ice," he said, peering sorrowfully through a film of lemonade.

"*Ben!* Do you have any idea how much work—" Melanie began.

"I'm sorry," he interrupted miserably. "It was an accident."

Melanie opened her mouth, then shut it abruptly, the dimples at the corners twitching convulsively. She seemed to be fighting for control even as her eyes crinkled with mirth. "I can't do it!" she exclaimed finally, starting to laugh. "I ought to be mad, but you look so *funny!*"

"I do?" Ben asked hopefully. A moment later the entire group was howling with laughter, Ben included.

"Peter doesn't look so great either," Ben pointed out proudly when the laughter had died down.

"You're right," said Peter. "Let's go see if we can find a hose and rinse ourselves off."

"Hurry!" Jenna called as the two of them ran off across the lawn. "They're opening the gates!"

"I'll have four . . . no, three . . . no, *four* hamburgers. And three Cokes," the little redheaded girl at the counter announced.

Leah took the girl's order, noting with relief that for once there was no one else standing in line. Team Take-out had been busy beyond belief ever since the carnival had opened, and Leah was ready for a few free minutes to catch her breath.

"Four burgers," Leah yelled back over her shoulder to Miguel. "We don't have Coke," she told the girl. "Is lemonade okay?"

The girl made a pouty face. "I guess."

"Three lemonades," Leah called to Ben as Jenna collected the money.

Ben rushed to fill the paper cups with ice, then began draining lemonade into them out of the spigot at the base of the vat. Leah watched with amusement as he filled one cup at a time, carrying each of them to the front counter as carefully as if it were full of nitroglycerin. Thanks to Ben, there was probably more lemonade in the grass than anywhere else, but for the last hour or so he'd been pretty good about keeping it in the cups. Even so, Leah's sneakers squished in nasty, sugary mud as she walked over to check on the burgers.

"How's it going back here?" she asked Miguel. "All we can see from up front is a cloud of smoke and a couple of flashing spatulas."

Miguel and Jesse had been cooking since the gates opened, while Melanie and Nicole helped with buns and plates. Leah, Ben, and Jenna had barely been able to leave the counter, and Peter had become the group's pinch hitter: he helped take orders, made more lemonade, ran to the cafeteria for ice and napkins, picked up the quarters Ben dropped in the grass, and just generally made himself indispensable.

"It's going good." Miguel seemed to be in high spirits as he waved his spatula in Jesse's direction. "We make a good team."

"That's right," Jesse yelled back. "Team Takeout! How much money have we made so far, Leah?"

"I haven't had time to count it, but a lot. The cash box is nearly full."

Miguel looked pleased. "The Englbehrts ought to be pretty happy. I wonder if they're here somewhere."

Something about the familiar way he mentioned Kurt's family caught Leah's attention. "Do you know them?" she asked.

He nodded, but before she could ask him how well, he changed the subject. "Who's got buns for these burgers?" he shouted.

Melanie scrambled to lay out plates and buns for four hamburgers and Miguel expertly added the meat.

"I'll take them over," Melanie offered, gathering up the full plates and walking toward the counter. It was the closest Leah had come to being alone with Miguel all day.

"It looks like it's starting to slow down," she said.

The little redhead was leaving with a man who was probably her father, and there was still no one else in line.

"Yeah. But hopefully it's only temporary. It's getting late for lunch, but in an hour or two people will start wanting dinner."

"Ugh. I'm not sure I'll ever be able to face food again," Leah joked, smiling. "I think I'll see hot dogs in my dreams."

Miguel smiled back and it was like that day in the hall all over again. His eyes held hers as if she were fascinating, as if there were nobody there but her. And Leah had to admit he intrigued her, too. Whatever his earlier problem with her had been, he seemed to be over it now. She met his gaze levelly, an unspoken challenge in her hazel eyes.

"Leah!" Ben wailed, shattering the moment. "Something's wrong with the ketchup dispenser."

Leah jumped, then winced. "I'm afraid to turn around," she whispered. "Tell me he's not wearing it."

Miguel chuckled and shook his head. "Sorry. But at least he knows where the hose is now."

"You're *kidding* . . . ," Leah began, spinning around. But the words died in her throat the instant she saw Ben.

Red goo dripped from his fingers and made a Rorschach test down the front of his busy shirt.

"I only wanted to see if we needed more ketchup," he said plaintively.

"I'll bet we need more now," Leah guessed.

"I'll go," Peter volunteered, running off toward the cafeteria.

"Look!" Jesse told Melanie, pointing with his hot dog tongs. "It's Kurt. Hey, Kurt!" he called, waving into the twilight.

Kurt spotted Jesse and waved back happily. Dana was with him, as always, but in place of the adoring smile she'd been wearing to school all week, the pretty blonde had a look of fatigue and strain. She held Kurt's hand tightly, almost fiercely. The unexpected protectiveness of the gesture reminded Melanie how sick he really was.

"Hey, Nicole, watch these dogs a minute, will you?" Jesse called, tossing her the tongs. Nicole hurried to relieve him, her grass skirt swishing. She'd kept it on after all, but with the shorts underneath and Jenna's too-large Hawaiian shirt knotted at her waist, it didn't look quite so ridiculous.

"Come on," Jesse urged, grabbing Melanie by the elbow. "Let's go say hi." The two of them headed toward the front of the booth, but Kurt was faster. He let go of Dana's hand and walked around the tables to meet them inside.

"Hey, Jesse! Thanks for coming out, man," he said, clapping his teammate on the shoulder. Dana remained outside the booth, a tight little smile on her lips.

"It's good to see you here," Jesse returned excitedly. "I didn't know if you'd be coming or not."

Kurt looked surprised. "Are you kidding? I wouldn't have missed this for anything! It's so incredible what you're all doing for me. Thanks, Jesse. I really mean it."

Jesse seemed suddenly embarrassed. "You remember Melanie, right?" he asked, pushing her forward.

"Who doesn't?" Kurt smiled and Melanie tried to smile back. Up close, Kurt looked even worse. His skin was pale and yellowed, and veins showed through in bluish blotches at his temples. Even so, something inside him seemed to shine out through his eyes. He looked sick, he looked weak, but he didn't look beaten. His expression was full of hope.

"Hey, Dana!" Kurt called. "Come say hello." Dana came reluctantly around the tables and took Kurt's hand again.

"Hi, Jesse. Hi, Melanie," she said, smiling briefly. Then she turned her attention back to her boyfriend. "Kurt, it's getting dark and you need to rest. Let's go find your parents, okay?"

"Since I've been sick, Dana acts more like my mom every day," Kurt told Jesse. His voice was light and teasing, but his expression as he looked at his girlfriend was so tender that Melanie's heart wrenched. *What would it be like to be loved that much?* she wondered enviously.

"I'm sorry," Dana apologized, turning to Melanie. "I try not to worry, but he . . . he's my best friend and . . ." Her voice choked up. "Well, you know how it is," she managed to say.

"Sure. I understand," Melanie said, feeling a strange ache down in her gut. "He's lucky to have you."

"Sure am," Kurt agreed, putting an arm across Dana's shoulders. "I couldn't have gotten through this without her."

"You're *not* through it, Kurt," Dana reminded him, a quiver in her voice. Her arm went around his waist and held on tight.

"Aw, come on, Dana. You know I'm going to beat this thing."

Dana nodded. "I know. I just wish you'd rest now."

"All right." Kurt smiled down at her and brushed the tip of her nose with one gentle finger. "If it means that much to you."

"Meet the rest of the group before you go," Jesse urged. "It'll only take a second."

"Sure!" Kurt agreed.

"Hey, everybody, come meet Kurt," Jesse called. The members of Team Take-out immediately abandoned their stations and crowded around the guest of honor.

"Miguel!" Kurt exclaimed as the group gathered

84

together. "I didn't see you back there! How's it going?" He stretched out a hand to Miguel, who stepped mutely forward to shake it. Then, as the rest of the group watched, Kurt pulled Miguel forward into a bear hug.

"This means a lot, man," he said huskily, patting Miguel on the back. Melanie was standing closest to them and she could barely make out the quiet words. "I know how hard this must be for you."

Miguel shook his head. "It's nothing," he said, his voice also strangely choked. "The least I could do." He returned Kurt's squeeze, then abruptly broke off the embrace and took a few steps backward into the growing darkness.

"Hi, Kurt," Peter said, stepping forward to fill the sudden silence. "I was sorry to hear about your leukemia, but I'm glad you're getting better. This is my best friend, Jenna."

"Right," Kurt said, smiling and looking from one to the other. "Thanks for coming out, you two."

Then Jesse introduced Kurt to Leah, Nicole, and Ben, and he shook each one's hand in turn. "I want you all to know how much I appreciate your support," he said sincerely. "It's been overwhelming."

"If there's anything else we can do to help you, you just let us know," Peter told him. "I mean it. Anything, anytime."

"Our pastor is going to take up a special collection at church tomorrow," Jenna added. "I know

85

our congregation would help in other ways, too, if there was something we could do."

Kurt seemed touched. He reached for Dana's hand and pulled her close to his side, then stood blinking rapidly in the failing light. "You could pray for me," he said at last.

"Okay, so what does that come out to?" Jesse asked Nicole. He was sitting on the grass near the Team Take-out booth, straightening the piles of ones, fives, tens, and twenties in the cash box while Leah finished wrapping the last roll of quarters. The rest of the group crowded around them in the brilliant artificial light of the stadium, eager to hear the final results.

Nicole wrote down the amounts from all five columns and did some quick addition on the pad of paper she held. She looked up from her figures and paused dramatically, enjoying the group's undivided attention. "Nine hundred, ninety-four dollars and fifty cents," she announced proudly.

"Wow!" Ben exclaimed. "That's a lot!"

Everyone murmured excited agreement until Miguel stepped forward, took out his wallet, and dropped some money on the pile. "Make it an even thousand," he said.

Jesse beamed as he added Miguel's contribution to the cash he'd already counted. "Thanks, man. Good idea."

"I can't believe we made so much money!" Jenna exclaimed.

"I know." Leah got up from the grass, pulling Jesse up behind her. "I feel really good about what we did here today."

The others nodded agreement with happy, satisfied faces, and no one said anything else for a few seconds. They simply stood there, absorbing their accomplishment. Then Jesse smiled and passed the cash box to Miguel. Miguel handed it to Leah. Leah gave it to Ben. It traveled the circle, passed from hand to hand, and for a moment Nicole felt a strong, unspoken bond connecting them all. They knew they were truly a team.

"Three cheers for Team Take-out!" Melanie cried suddenly, disrupting the silence. "Hip, hip . . ."

"Hooray!" the rest of them shouted.

"Hip, hip . . ."

"Hooray!"

"Hip, hip . . ."

"Hooray!"

It was a very cheerleader-y thing to do, but under the circumstances, Nicole not only forgave her rival, she joined in.

"That much money ought to help Kurt a lot," Miguel said a little wistfully as the cheer died down.

"I'll be praying that it does," Peter said sincerely.

Jenna nodded. "Me too."

Nicole shifted her feet uneasily, uncomfortable

with so much talk about praying. First Kurt, and now Peter and Jenna . . . Praying was all well and good, but did they need to discuss it in public? She winced at the thought of what Courtney would say. Courtney's family didn't go to church, and Courtney never hesitated to tell anyone who'd listen that religion was "a total waste of time."

"Yeah, well, that's great," said Jesse, sounding as uncomfortable as Nicole felt.

"We'd better get started cleaning up this mess if we don't want to be here until tomorrow," Miguel put in, mercifully changing the subject.

"He's right," said Leah. "Someone should take the money over to the office now, and the rest of us can start tearing down this booth and getting things washed up."

"Melanie and I'll go turn in the money," Jesse said. "That's fair, since we were the booth leaders."

"I've got to wash the lemonade container!" Melanie protested. "And there's all that other stuff in the gym to wash, too. You don't need me to go with you."

"Well, I guess not. . . ."

Nicole thought Jesse looked much too disappointed. "I'll go with you, Jesse," she said. "I mean, if you don't want to go by yourself."

"Well . . ."

"Yeah, take Nicole," Melanie told him. "You guys

can carry some of those extra boxes of buns to the cafeteria on your way."

"Okay!" Nicole agreed eagerly, hurrying to grab a box. The next thing she knew, she was walking through the warm night air, alone at last with Jesse Jones.

The carnival was breaking down all around them as they took a shortcut across the field and under the "away" bleachers. Other students hurried back and forth on their various errands, but Nicole barely saw them. Instead she cast glance after furtive glance at Jesse, wishing he'd say something, trying to decide if she should. She hugged the cardboard bun box to her chest and berated herself for not thinking of a plan in advance. After all, wasn't this the opportunity she'd waited for all week—her entire reason for signing up for the carnival in the first place?

"I'm glad you were on my team today, Nicole," Jesse said suddenly, out of the blue. "It was a big help having you setting up those plates."

"Well, I, uh—I'm glad, too," Nicole stammered, caught off guard. "It was fun."

Jesse turned to look at her, a thoughtful smile on his perfect lips. "It was, wasn't it? We made a good team."

"We made a *great* team," she said enthusiastically. Then, seeing her chance, she added, "We ought to do something else together sometime."

Jesse seemed to consider her suggestion. "I don't know what else we could do. It was fine for the carnival, but everyone in the group is so different . . . I can't really see us hanging out together."

He had totally misunderstood her. Did she dare to set him straight? Nicole's heart was racing and way too much adrenaline pounded through her veins, but she knew she'd never have a better chance to say how she felt. She took a deep breath and went for it. "No. I meant you and *I* should do something together sometime."

"*Us?* Like what?"

"I don't know. Do you like to go to the movies?" Was her voice shaking, she wondered, or was that just the blood in her ears?

"Are you talking about a date?" Jesse asked, his expression amused. "It sounds like you're asking me out."

Was he laughing at her? Had she totally blown it? Nicole felt like a possum caught in the headlights, about to be run over. "No, of course not," she lied, panicking.

"Oh."

And all the way to the cafeteria, he didn't say anything else.

Six

" ' Amazing grace, how sweet the sound . . . ,' " Jenna sang, her soprano voice lifting high above the others. She looked forward to singing in church all week, but it felt especially good this morning, when she had so much to be thankful for.

The carnival for Kurt Englbehrt had been a huge success, and Jenna was happy she'd had the chance to meet him and let him know they were praying for him. Reverend Thompson had already told the congregation about Kurt and taken the special collection, so now there was even more money to help him. *I just know Kurt's going to get well*, she thought as she sang the hymn. *He has to now.* Joy bubbled up inside her, making her want to sing even more. Making a difference, truly helping someone, felt fantastic.

Jenna looked down at her mother, blissfully leading the choir, and her heart gave a little tug. She was so happy, so lucky to have the life she did. Her glance wandered to the pews, to her dad sitting in front with her four at-home sisters. Shy Caitlin sat directly next to her father, then Maggie and

Allison, with Sarah on the end. Sarah saw her looking and waved, but Allison pulled her younger sister's hand down, whispering obvious disapproval. Sarah paused, chastened, then brightened and waved with her other hand, the one Allison couldn't reach. Jenna looked away quickly, before her sisters could make her laugh and ruin the song.

Her eyes sought out Peter on the other side of the church. He and his parents were sitting with Chris Hobart, from the Junior Explorers program, and Chris's girlfriend, Maura Kennedy. Peter was the only person in his group who wasn't singing, Jenna noted, undoubtedly out of consideration for the rest of the congregation. He smiled when he saw her looking his way and nodded his hello.

The song came to an end, and Mrs. Conrad gave the signal for the choir to be seated. Jenna sat down carefully, trying not to crease her robe, as Reverend Thompson began his final remarks.

Because of the collection for Kurt, the sermon had been about the need for people to love and help each other. The reverend now closed with a reading from the Book of Matthew.

"Then the King will say to those on his right, 'Come, you who are blessed by my Father; take your inheritance, the kingdom prepared for you since the creation of the world. For I was hungry and you gave me something to eat, I was thirsty and you gave me something to drink, I was a stranger and you invited me in, I needed clothes and you clothed me, I was sick and you looked after me, I was in prison and you came to visit me.'

"Then the righteous will answer him, 'Lord, when did we see you hungry and feed you, or thirsty and give you something to drink? When did we see you a stranger and invite you in, or needing clothes and clothe you? When did we see you sick or in prison and go to visit you?'

"The King will reply, 'I tell you the truth, whatever you did for one of the least of these brothers of mine, you did for me.' "

The organist took over then, and the choir rose and began filing out. Jenna reflected on the Bible verses as she walked, and once again felt an overwhelming gladness at having been able to help Kurt Englbehrt.

Not only that, but it had been fun working with Team Take-out, the whole group pitching in together. Jenna's only teeny-tiny regret was that she hadn't had a chance to spend any real time with Miguel. Of course she'd taken a few seconds out of her busy day to notice how handsome he'd looked in his Hawaiian shirt. She'd also noticed that he'd worked like four men behind that hamburger grill—as if he were driven somehow. But Jenna had spent the day at the front counter and Miguel at the back of the booth, nowhere near each other until everyone gathered together at the end.

Jenna smiled. At least they were on a first-name basis now. Starting tomorrow, she could talk to him in homeroom.

To every thing there is a season, and a time to every purpose under the heaven, Jenna thought happily, reaching back in her memory for a Bible verse of her own.

"Oh, it feels good just to lie here and not worry about that stupid carnival anymore," Vanessa Winters declared, stretching out more comfortably on her lounge chair next to the Andrewses' swimming pool. The bikini she wore was red and slinky, and her pale skin glistened beneath a coat of baby oil. "Thank God it's over."

"You're not kidding," said Lou Anne. "I hope Kurt appreciates it."

It seemed heartless to talk about Kurt that way when he was still so sick, but Melanie had to admit that she'd been thinking along the same lines the night before when she'd invited the cheering squad over for an impromptu pool party. Instead of the relief she'd anticipated feeling, though, Melanie's thoughts kept returning to the worried way Dana had clung to Kurt's hand at the carnival. She hoped he'd get well soon.

"I'm sure he does," Cindy White replied dismissively. "Hey, Tiffany, can I use some of your suntan oil? It smells good."

Tiffany sat up on her lounge chair, a sour expression on her delicate face. "Why didn't you bring your own? Mine's too expensive to be passing around."

"Use mine," Melanie said quickly, tossing the brown plastic bottle to Cindy.

"Thanks." Cindy threw an annoyed glance at Tiffany before sitting up to oil her legs.

There were eight cheerleaders on the CCHS squad, including Melanie, and six of them were there that day. Sue and Angela had standing Sunday plans with their families and had turned down Melanie's last-minute invitation, but the other five had come: Vanessa, Lou Anne, Cindy, Tiffany, and Tanya. They'd arrived at Melanie's house at noon and set up lounge chairs around Melanie's enormous pool, looking forward to a little sun and relaxation.

And the weather hadn't disappointed them—it was hot, clear, and gorgeous. The cheerleaders reclined like princesses on their lounges, surrounded by a confusion of extra towels, suntan oil, bottled water, magazines, and sweating cans of ice-cold soda. Beside them, the rectangular swimming pool sparkled in the sun, reflecting the back side of the Andrewses' unusual glass-and-concrete home. Soft music played through the poolside speakers, adding to the illusion that the six of them were on an island somewhere, far away from the regular world.

"You sure have a beautiful house," Tanya told Melanie, rolling over on her lounge chair to face her. "I'd kill to have a pool like this."

"Thanks," said Melanie.

"If *you* had a pool like this," Tiffany butted in, "no one would be able to use it. No one *human*, that is. Those bratty little brothers of yours would splash everyone."

Tanya's hazel eyes flashed dangerously.

"You'll have to bring your brothers over sometime," Melanie interceded quickly. "If you think they'd like to come."

Tanya shot Tiffany one last dirty look, then turned to smile at Melanie, her teeth white against the dark brown of her cheeks. "They *will* splash you," she admitted. "But they'd love to swim in this pool. And your house will amaze them—they'll think it's a castle."

"It *is* a castle," Lou Anne declared.

"Yeah, what's the story, Melanie?" Cindy asked. "Are you guys loaded, or what?"

Melanie winced, then chose her words carefully. "We do all right. The house was important to my parents—kind of a project of theirs. My mom was a painter, and my dad was pretty high up in his mining company before he retired last year. He could afford to let Mom's imagination run a little wild."

96

"By the way, where *is* your mom?" Tiffany asked. "I can't believe that neither one of your parents has been out here to bug us the entire time."

"Tiff!" Cindy whispered, aghast. An uneasy hush settled over the group.

"What?" Tiffany was still looking at Melanie.

"My . . . uh . . . my mother died," Melanie managed, hating the other girl for making her say it out loud. "I thought you all knew that."

"Oh, *that's* right," Tiffany acknowledged with a giggle. "I forgot."

Sure you did, Melanie thought, knowing she'd never be able to look at Tiffany again without remembering this moment. Her vision blurred with hurt, angry tears, and she was suddenly terrified she wouldn't be able to hide them. She turned her head away and closed her eyes, willing them back with all her might. She would *not* cry in front of these girls—not now, not ever.

"Hey, Melanie," Tanya said, "if it's not too much trouble, could I have another Coke?"

Melanie nodded and scrambled out of her lounge chair, hurrying over the pool deck toward the house. She wasn't even through the kitchen door when the tears started sliding down her cheeks, but at least she was out of sight. She'd have to thank Tanya someday—she knew the other girl had only asked for the soda to give her an excuse to leave.

The interior of the big concrete house was cool

and silent. Melanie walked blindly through the large, modern kitchen on her way to the nearest downstairs bathroom. The face that looked back at her from the mirror above the sink seemed somehow pale beneath its tan, and her green eyes were wet, the pupils dilated. Turning on the cold water, Melanie splashed her face repeatedly, rhythmically, until she finally forgot why she was doing it. Then she straightened up and dried her face on a hand towel, took down her hair and rebrushed it into its ponytail, and put on new mascara and lip gloss. *There, you can't even tell now*, she thought, surveying her frozen reflection.

Back in the kitchen, she opened the industrial-sized stainless-steel refrigerator and began loading sodas onto a tray. The air spilling from the large compartment was cold on her bare skin, most of which was exposed by her white bikini, and she hurried to finish. She had just closed the door again and was lifting the loaded tray when her father stumbled in from the living room.

As usual, he looked terrible. His watery blue eyes were puffy and bloodshot, his wavy brown hair was uncombed, and an aggressive growth of brown and silver stubble peppered his cheeks and chin. He was wearing a ratty old plaid bathrobe tied on over boxer shorts, and his skinny, dead-white feet seemed lost in their stretched-out slippers.

"What are you doing, Mel, sweetie?" he asked, glancing at her full tray. "You must be awfully thirsty."

And thirsty is the last thing you are, Melanie thought, smelling the familiar reek of alcohol on his breath. "I have some friends over, Dad," was all she said.

"Really? That's nice." Mr. Andrews shuffled unsteadily over to a window and looked out at the backyard. He was plenty drunk, and he gripped the windowsill for support. "Who *are* those girls?"

"They're the other cheerleaders. Well, most of them, anyway. Two couldn't make it."

Melanie's dad nodded, as if to say he knew all about the other cheerleaders, even though he'd never seen any of them before. "Why didn't you tell me they were coming?"

"Does it matter?"

"No."

"That's why." The tray of drinks in her hands was starting to get heavy. Melanie set it back down on the counter.

"Maybe I should come out and say hello to your friends," Mr. Andrews suggested. "I could order you girls some pizzas if you want."

"No, that's okay. Why don't you go back to the den and lie down for a while?"

"Don't you think I should go out there?" he asked wistfully. He turned around to face her. "Don't you want me to, Mel?"

"Of course I want you to. But you'd have to shower and shave and put on some clothes, and I just can't see you doing that right now. You can meet the girls another time, when you feel more up to it."

"I'm up to it, Mel . . . ," Mr. Andrews began, then lost his train of thought. He stood immobile near the kitchen window, trying to remember something . . . anything. "What time is it?" he asked suddenly.

"Time for you to lie down, Dad. Come on."

Melanie helped her father into the den around the corner from the living room, where he liked to sleep on the now ruined sofa. She flipped the TV on and turned the volume down low, then went to the hall closet for a blanket. When she returned a minute later, Mr. Andrews was already passed out, snoring softly on his back. Melanie spread the blanket over the man who used to be her father, trying not to think, not to feel.

In the first weeks after her mother had been killed, Melanie had gone to grief counseling. "I know it's hard," the psychiatrist had told her, "but it'll get easier as time goes by."

That had been two years ago, and Melanie knew for sure now that the psychiatrist had been wrong. It was getting harder. Harder every day.

"How was your afternoon at the club?" Jesse's stepmother asked as he pulled out a chair at the dinner table Sunday evening.

Jesse opened his mouth to tell her, but she'd already lost interest, turning instead to her twelve-year-old daughter. "Brittany, darling, more salad and less bread and butter. We don't want to get fat, do we?"

Brittany looked appalled at the mere thought and tossed a roll back into the breadbasket. "I don't know what difference it makes," she complained. "I could be thin as a bone and no one would even know it with those horrible jumpers they make us wear at Sacred Heart."

"I know, sweetheart," the new Mrs. Jones said sympathetically. "You know I'd do something about it if I could, but the sisters aren't particularly concerned about fashion—"

"Obviously," Brittany interrupted with a snigger. "Look how *they* dress."

"Now, Brittany . . ."

Jesse tuned out the sound of his snobby, socialite stepmother trying to appease his disgustingly spoiled little stepsister. He heard the jumper debate at least once a week, and he was sick to death of it. "What did you do today, Dad?" he asked, snapping the other member of the family out of his stupor.

"What? Oh. Your mother and I did some shopping in the morning. Then in the afternoon I worked on my article for the medical journal."

My mother—that's a hot one, Jesse thought. His real mother still lived in California, and his two real brothers were grown up and away at Princeton and MIT. Meanwhile, he was stuck in the sticks of Missouri with his clueless doctor father, a gold-digging Barbie look-alike half his age, and her clone-in-training daughter. *The only thing real about this family is the pain in the butt it gives me.*

But he didn't say that, of course. He never did.

"Did you win today?" Jesse's father asked.

"Huh? Oh, yeah." Jesse had been playing tennis at the country club. He didn't much like tennis—as a sport, it couldn't hold a candle to football—but he'd always been good at it.

"You ought to join the tennis team at school," Jesse's stepmother put in. "You could probably be the captain."

Jesse tried to keep the disgust off his face. None of the guys at school even knew he played a sissy sport like tennis. "I'm on the football team, Elsa."

"But you're not the *captain*," Brittany pointed out, looking to her mother for an approving smile.

"All in good time, B. Someday you'll be watching me on Monday Night Football."

Brittany looked skeptical, but hopeful. Jesse knew that despite all her posturing, she really looked up to him. After all, he was the only brother she'd ever had—and a good-looking older brother at that. Every time she had one of her stupid slumber parties all her little friends followed him around the house with stars in their eyes, telling her how lucky she was.

"You'd be a lot less likely to get hurt playing tennis," Elsa said.

"Your mother's right," Dr. Jones agreed. "I was reading something in a medical journal the other day about a football player whose vertebrae were so compressed that . . ."

Jesse tuned him out and shoveled down the rest of his dinner. By now he'd heard more football horror stories than complaints about Brittany's stupid school uniform. If he didn't get away from these people, he was going to go crazy.

"That was a great dinner, Elsa," he said, interrupting his father halfway through a description of the X rays. "I've, uh, got somewhere to go now, though, and if I don't hurry I'll be late. See you all later."

He'd taken them by surprise, and he got away clean, hurrying toward the garage. The huge triple door rose with a mechanical hum when Jesse punched the button, and a moment later he was out on the road, driving his BMW.

He had lied about having somewhere to go.

Jesse cruised the streets aimlessly, his headlights raking the darkness. It wasn't so bad living with Elsa and his dad, but it wasn't so great, either. If his father hadn't accepted that stupid research position and moved them all to Missouri, it could have been a lot better. Jesse thought back to when he was younger and his parents were still together. His brothers had been at home then, and the whole family had lived in a killer house in Malibu, right on the sand. They'd had such good times: Christmases, birthdays, summers on the beach.

Jesse missed the ocean.

Or, no. Maybe it was his mother, or his brothers, or his friends back in California that he missed. He missed *something*. His whole life felt so scattered now—nothing he did seemed to make any difference. The way his group had dominated at the carnival had made him feel great, but it hadn't lasted. For a while there, when Kurt and Dana had come over and thanked him, all the hard work he'd put in had seemed well worth it. But here it was, only a day later, and everything already seemed hollow and pointless again. It was like that now. Nothing ever lasted for him.

Jesse came to a crossroads and turned right, deciding to cruise past Melanie's house.

Melanie. There was a subject all by itself.

Why did he waste his time on Melanie Andrews when practically any other girl at school would be happy to have him for a boyfriend? He didn't understand her. One minute she'd lead him on, sweet as could be, and the next she'd turn around and insult him.

That's why, he suddenly realized.

Jesse didn't even know if he really liked Melanie, but he definitely welcomed the distraction.

Dear *Clearwater Crossing* Reader,

Your opinion counts! Please answer the following questions and return this card after you have read the book. Be completely honest—there are no right or wrong answers. No stamp is necessary, just drop the card in any mailbox. Thanks!

≋ clearwater crossing ≋

1. Did you like this book? (Check one) ☐ I loved it ☐ I liked it ☐ It was OK ☐ I didn't like it ☐ I hated it

2. How did you find out about this book? (Check one) ☐ Teen magazine ☐ Brio magazine ☐ In-store sampler ☐ Radio advertisements ☐ Bookstore ☐ In-store Display
☐ Ad in a Lurlene McDaniel book ☐ Ad in a Love Stories book ☐ Friend ☐ Other (Please specify)

3. Would you read another *Clearwater Crossing* book? (Check one) ☐ Definitely Yes ☐ Probably Yes ☐ Maybe ☐ Probably Not ☐ Definitely Not

4. Please rank the following in order of importance to you in deciding to buy this book (1 being most important, 6 being least):
____ Subject/content ____ Cover ____ Friend recommended ____ Back of book copy ____ Read preview sampler ____ Advertisement

5. Would you recommend *Clearwater Crossing* to a friend? (Check one) ☐ Definitely Yes ☐ Probably Yes ☐ Maybe ☐ Probably Not ☐ Definitely Not

6. Where did you buy this book? ☐ Walden ☐ Borders ☐ Barnes & Noble ☐ Religious bookstore (Store name) _____
☐ Discount store (like K-Mart) ☐ Grocery store ☐ Received as a gift ☐ Other (Please specify) _____ ☐ Other bookstore

7. Who picked out this book? (Check one) ☐ I did ☐ Friend ☐ Parent/Grandparent ☐ Other (Please specify) _____

8. Who paid for this book? (Check one) ☐ I did ☐ Friend ☐ Parent/Grandparent ☐ Other (Please specify) _____

9. Which of these books/series do you like to read? (Check all that apply) ☐ Lurlene McDaniel ☐ PCU ☐ Chrissy ☐ Cedar River Daydreams ☐ Sierra Jensen
☐ Love Stories ☐ Other _____

10. Do you belong to a Christian or church youth group? ☐ Yes ☐ No If yes, what is the name of the group? _____

11. On a scale of 1-10 (1 is worst, 10 is best), how does *Clearwater Crossing* rank as a series? _____

12. Which, if any, of these magazines do you read regularly? (Check all that apply) ☐ YM ☐ Teen ☐ Brio ☐ Seventeen ☐ You! ☐ Youth 97

Reader's Name _____

Address _____ City _____ State _____ Zip _____

Date of Birth ____ / ____ / ____

CCS#1

Seven

From the desk of Principal Kelly
(Teachers: Please read in homeroom.)

Good morning, students!

I have outstanding news to share with you all on this beautiful Tuesday. Kurt Englbehrt had a broad series of tests performed yesterday, and his doctors have pronounced him in remission! Let me say again how proud I am of the way this school rallied around Kurt and his family in their time of need.

On a less enthusiastic note, I want to remind you all that smoking in the bathrooms is a good way to get suspended. Just don't do it.

Also, the CCHS Wildcats will be playing their first football game of the season on Friday, against the Springville Muskrats. I urge you all to turn out and support your team.

Go, Wildcats!

"Isn't it great about Kurt?" Jenna asked, smiling at Peter. "I'm so happy for him." They were sitting at one of the round lunch tables outside the cafeteria, and so far they had it to themselves.

Peter returned her smile. "Incredible. My whole class cheered when Mr. Taylor read the announcement."

"I can't wait to tell my parents. And Reverend Thompson. Everyone's going to be so excited to hear how our prayers were answered." Jenna finished laying out her brown-bag lunch of yogurt, chips, and a salami sandwich—the same thing she ate every Tuesday—and wished she'd put some cookies in too.

"Hey! Hi, you guys!" someone yelled suddenly, practically in Jenna's ear. The unexpected noise made her jump, and her knees hit the underside of the table, upsetting her orange juice in a spectacular splash. The sticky orange puddle spread quickly on the faded plastic table, most of it running directly toward Peter.

"Oops. Sorry, Jenna," murmured the voice that had bellowed only moments before. It was Ben Pipkin. She should have guessed.

"No problem. I've got it under control," Peter said, tossing napkins onto the flood. "How's it going, Ben?"

"I . . . um . . . okay, I guess." Ben's earlier excitement at seeing them had been replaced by his normal state of embarrassment.

He's almost painful to be around, Jenna thought, dabbing at her side of the table with one insignificant paper napkin. Being nice to Ben was starting to take a toll on her sense of humor.

"Let me buy you another orange juice, Jenna," Ben offered.

"No, that's . . . ," Jenna began, but Ben was already running off toward the cafeteria.

"Get more napkins!" Peter called after him.

"Can you believe that guy?" Jenna asked, tossing her sopping napkin into a nearby trash can, along with her sodden corn chips. "I've never met anyone so clumsy in my life!"

Peter's eyes twinkled. "*You* spilled the juice."

"Thanks for reminding me," Jenna said grumpily. "I mean it, Peter. He wears me out."

"He's probably just happy to finally know someone to sit with. It must be pretty lonely eating by himself all the time."

"I know, and I feel sorry for him, but why does he have to sit with *us?*"

"We said we'd be nice to him, remember?" Peter looked vaguely disturbed. "Why are you acting this way?"

"I . . . I don't know," Jenna murmured, suddenly ashamed of herself. "I guess I just look forward to eating lunch with you. Alone. I like to be able to talk privately."

"So you're finally realizing how much you take me for granted," Peter teased. But then he turned serious. "I look forward to eating with you too, Jenna. Don't worry. This won't be a regular thing."

Jenna smiled and their gazes locked in silent understanding.

"I'm back!" Ben announced loudly, running up behind her again. This time Jenna barely flinched. "I got you another orange juice, and some cookies too, Jenna." Ben pushed his purchases into her hands, then pulled a stack of crumpled napkins from his pocket and started swiping awkwardly at the juice. Peter pitched in to help, and eventually they all sat down together at a reasonably dry table.

"Thanks for the cookies, Ben," said Jenna. "How did you know I was dying for some?"

Ben's answering smile was enormous. His magnified eyes glowed behind their Coke-bottle lenses. "I guessed," he said proudly. "You looked like a cookie girl to me."

Jenna's eyebrows hit her hairline. Was Ben saying she was fat? She knew she had a few extra pounds, but she usually felt fine about the way she looked. No one had ever been rude enough to mention her weight before. "I'm not sure that's a compliment, Ben," she said slowly. "How does a cookie girl look?"

Ben seemed puzzled by the question. "Well . . . like you, Jenna. You know . . . kind of wholesome."

Peter chuckled. "That's Jenna. Wholesome."

Jenna tossed her long brown hair. "I *am* wholesome, thank you very much." She ripped open the bag of bite-sized cookies and popped one into her mouth.

The rest of the lunch period flew by. Ben talked and talked, as if he'd been stranded on a desert island and had only just reached civilization again. The surprising thing was that once he calmed down and started to relax, he was funny.

He told them about his software-programming father, a computer genius so involved in his work that the week before he'd gotten up with a brainstorm in the middle of the night, thrown a robe on over his pajamas, and run to the computer in the den to hack out a new program. By the time it started getting light, he was so eager to log on to the souped-up computer at his office that he'd downloaded his work onto a portable hard drive and run out the door with it. It wasn't until his colleagues started showing up later that morning that Mr. Pipkin realized he'd forgotten to get dressed. Not only that, but the bathrobe he was wearing turned out to be a hot pink number belonging to *Mrs.* Pipkin.

"And my mother is, uh, a *large* woman," Ben said, concluding his story.

"Your poor father! He must have been mortified!"

Jenna gasped through peals of laughter. She could practically see an older version of Ben running around clueless in an enormous, fluffy pink robe.

"Nah, not him." Ben shook his head. "If they'd let him, he'd probably just have taken off the robe and worked in his pajamas all day. My *mom* was pretty ticked off, though. She didn't like the idea of everyone at ComAm seeing her lingerie."

"I guess not!" Jenna agreed. She would have said more, but the bell for fifth period rang just then, breaking up their discussion.

"Oops! I've got to hurry," said Ben. "I've got gym this period, and if I don't get to the locker room and change before the other guys come in, they take my shorts."

"Nice guys!" Jenna said indignantly.

Ben shrugged. "Anyway, thanks for letting me eat with you. It was fun."

"Anytime," Jenna returned, surprising herself.

Ben smiled shyly as he shouldered his backpack. Then he turned and sprinted off toward the gym.

"Come on," said Peter. "I'll walk you to choir practice."

"That's okay. You've got chemistry."

"No, I want to," Peter insisted.

"What for?"

Peter never walked her to her classes. That was the kind of thing couples did, not friends.

"I just want to, okay? I hardly even got to talk to you at lunch."

"Okay." Jenna picked up her books and headed for the main building, Peter at her side. If Peter wanted to start walking her to classes all of a sudden, it was no big deal.

It was just weird.

"When, uh, when Darwin was voyaging aboard the H.M.S. *Beagle*, he noticed all of the different, unique species in the Galápagos Islands. Uh, that is to say that each of the islands had unique species. And that, um, well, it started him thinking about populations in isolation. . . ." Ms. Walker's voice as she stumbled through her Tuesday-afternoon biology lecture was low and extremely nervous.

Leah glanced toward the front of the room and saw the teacher eyeing her warily, as if she expected Leah to contradict her at any second. But Leah had no such intention. For one thing, she'd already made her point. For another, she was starting to find watching Miguel del Rios far more compelling than listening to Ms. Walker's uninspired lectures.

It had seemed as if she and Miguel had really clicked at the carnival. There had been that one moment in particular at the grill when their eyes caught and held. Then later, when everyone was cleaning up, Miguel had been almost chatty. He'd seemed really excited that their group had done so well, and kept saying what a big help the money would be to Kurt and his family. Leah had never managed to get him alone long enough to question him further about his friendship with Kurt, but, judging by the heartfelt exchange she'd witnessed between the two of them, they must have been pretty close once. She only wished she'd been near enough to hear what they'd said to each other.

Leah had intended to ask Miguel more about Kurt on Monday after class, but so far this week he seemed to be compensating for Saturday's excess of enthusiasm by keeping more to himself than ever. He'd said hi to her yesterday, but that was about it. "Hi" had practically killed him.

She watched him now, bewildered, while their biology teacher droned on. Leah could only see the back of his head and a sliver of his profile, but even his hair seemed to be brooding. How could he be so sullen when the rest of the school was practically walking on air with the news of Kurt's recovery? Was the guy always this up and down? And if he didn't like to talk, why had he made such a special point of talking to *her*?

Leah sighed impatiently, unaware she had made a sound until poor Ms. Walker flinched.

"Oops! Oh, wow. Sorry." Melanie had been in such a rush to get to the bus stop that she'd run right into someone. All she'd seen as she'd rounded the corner of the gym was a glimpse of the navy blue T-shirt her face was buried in now. She backed away hurriedly, praying that by some miracle her victim wouldn't recognize her.

"Melanie!" said Peter Altmann.

"I . . . I . . . oh boy, do I ever feel stupid," she said, embarrassed. "Are you okay? Did I hurt you?"

Peter stared down at her a moment, his dark blond hair spilling across his startled blue eyes, before he started laughing. "Did you *hurt* me? No. And do my reputation a favor and don't tell anyone you did, all right? I get enough grief for being skinny without the whole school thinking the littlest cheerleader on the squad beat me up."

"Well . . . all right," Melanie agreed slowly, smiling. "If it will save your reputation, I guess we can keep this our secret."

"Thanks. You're all heart."

"Don't mention it."

They were still standing there, still smiling, but now that the joke was over, Melanie couldn't think of a single thing to say. Peter was looking at her expectantly, obviously waiting for her to start some sort of conversation, but her mind was a total blank. She suddenly realized that she'd made it from Sunday all the way to Wednesday without seeing or even thinking of Peter once. It was strange how long ago the carnival already seemed, and even stranger to see Peter on his own like this, now that there wasn't any reason for them to get together.

"It's great about Kurt, isn't it?" she said at last.

"Great," Peter agreed, beaming. "The best."

Another pause—this one longer and more uncomfortable. "So, uh, what are you doing here so late?" Melanie finally managed.

Peter pointed over his shoulder at the bulging pack on his back. "Checking out some books at the library. We have a major paper coming up in art appreciation. Have you taken that class?"

"No, but I want to. I'll probably take it next year."

Peter smiled. "It's a ton of work, but it's worth it. Try to get Mr. McIntosh—he's really good."

Melanie nodded awkwardly, unable to reply. *What's wrong with me?* she thought. *I worked with this guy all day on Saturday and I talked to him just fine then.*

"How about you?" Peter asked.

"Huh?"

"Why are *you* here so late?"

"Oh. Cheering practice." Melanie glanced down at her sweaty workout clothes, then rolled her eyes. "I'm embarrassed you even caught me like this, but when I stay to shower I miss the four o'clock bus."

"You look fine to me."

Another guy would have made it sound like a compliment. Or a come-on. From Peter it just sounded like a fact. He smiled at her as if to reinforce that interpretation.

"Yeah, well . . . thanks. But, uh, I should go. If I miss that bus I'll be here another hour."

"Okay," said Peter. "See you around."

"See ya."

Melanie trotted off toward the bus stop without looking back, her pulse unusually fast. She didn't know why, but the encounter with Peter had rattled her. She couldn't even remember the last time she'd had so much trouble making simple conversation with a guy—any guy.

It's only because we hang out in such different circles, Melanie told herself as she ran. *Not to mention that nearly knocking someone down isn't the world's greatest way to break the ice. Of course I couldn't think of anything to say after that.*

She reached the bus stop just as the bus pulled up, and she swung herself aboard. There was an empty seat near the front and she dropped into it gratefully.

We have nothing in common, that's the problem. And besides, Peter seems awfully religious. He'd probably be horrified if he knew about some of the things I've done.

On Saturday afternoon it had finally occurred to Melanie that the pewter fish Peter was wearing around his neck was a Christian symbol. His best friend, Jenna, usually wore a cross. Not only that, but Melanie remembered the expression on Peter's face when he'd promised to pray for Kurt. She'd known right then that he wasn't just saying it, that he fully intended to do it. There was something about Peter that was completely genuine. *Maybe that's why I don't know what to say to him*, Melanie thought. *I'm afraid he's actually listening.*

When Melanie was younger, she'd gone to Sunday school with friends a few times. But that was before she'd understood why those trips always involved other people's families. Later she'd found out. Melanie's mother used to say that if God existed he wouldn't be at any church *she'd* ever visited, and Melanie's father was an atheist. In fact, in the whole world there were only two subjects Melanie didn't dare mention to her dad: God and her mother's death.

The bus dropped her off on her street at last, and Melanie stepped into the silent entryway of her house, scanning the empty concrete walls. Once, a couple of years ago, all that cold raw concrete had been covered with her mother's watercolors. Beautiful paintings, full of color and life—a collection of images that had given the house soul. But now they were gone. Her father had had them taken down and exiled to a storeroom when her mother died. He couldn't look at them, he'd said. Seeing them hurt too much.

And this doesn't hurt? Melanie thought. *Denying*

that Mom even existed? Never, ever, talking about what happened?

With a sigh, she dropped her book bag at the bottom of the stairs and walked through the house to the den. As she'd expected, her dad was passed out on the couch again, the TV a barely audible drone in the background. She remembered when he'd been different—when he'd cared about her, about living. But the last two years had seen a slow, sad falling apart. First he'd started drinking, then he'd quit his job, then he'd stopped getting dressed in the morning. It was all he could do now to pay the bills and keep Mrs. Murphy and their other help on a schedule. Melanie knew he was dying from the inside out, just the way she was. It was kind of funny how hard they both worked to keep those deaths a secret.

For no apparent reason, Melanie suddenly remembered Peter Altmann's smile. *It would have been nice if we could have been friends*, she thought, knowing it would never happen.

"That's not possible!" Nicole whispered under her breath. She stepped off the bathroom scale and waited for the dial to stop spinning, then, slowly, carefully, stepped back on. The numbers passed giddily under the needle, coming to rest in the exact same spot. She'd gained a pound!

"How could I be so *disgusting?*" she moaned. "No

117

wonder guys don't like me!" Her eyes filled with frustrated, disappointed tears, blurring the numbers between her feet.

Ever since she'd humiliated herself by dropping those obvious hints on Saturday, Jesse had barely looked at her. Monday she hadn't been *too* worried; Tuesday it had bothered her more; Wednesday she'd obsessed about it; and after today, Thursday, she knew that she'd totally blown it. How could she have been so *stupid*? She should have let *him* come to *her*!

But he wasn't *coming to you,* Nicole reminded herself bitterly. *The only person he even knows exists is stupid Melanie Andrews.*

More tears blurred her vision, dripping down onto the scale. Nicole shivered in her underwear but stayed where she was, punishing herself for her loss of control. She *deserved* to suffer. At this rate, she was going to be a blimp! A *fat, ugly blimp that no one will ever*—

The door suddenly flew open on Heather's side of the bathroom. "Oops! Sorry," Heather said. "I didn't know you were in here and I really have to . . . are you *crying?*"

Nicole grabbed for a towel and clutched it to her half-naked body. "Get *out* of here, Heather!"

"What are you crying for?" Heather demanded, not budging.

"Nothing. None of your business. Now, *leave.*"

"If you don't tell me, I'm calling Mom. This is my bathroom, too, Nicole. I have a right to use it when I want to."

"Not if I'm in here first, you don't! Can't you see I'm busy?"

"No. All I see is you standing on the scale in your underwear. I swear you're on that thing every five minutes."

"I happen to care how I look. . . ." But the indignity of being barged in on, on top of gaining a pound and blowing it with Jesse and everything else, was more than Nicole could take. Tears welled up again. Why should she explain herself to Heather, anyway?

"Forget it. You can have the bathroom," she said, turning around and hurrying back into her bedroom. She rushed to close the door on her side, but Heather was right behind her, blocking the doorway.

"You're crying because of the *scale*, aren't you?" she asked incredulously. "You're crying because you gained weight."

"Only a pound!" Nicole shrieked. "You shut up!"

Heather's gray eyes widened with disgusted amazement. "And you're crying? How vain can you be, Nicole?" She shook her head. "You *really* need to get a life."

"I'll get a life when I'm good and ready!" Nicole shouted furiously, wrestling with the door until she finally forced it closed. She could hear Heather

119

laughing on the other side, and for a moment she seriously considered going back in there and shutting her up. How dare Heather walk in on her like that, and how *dare* she tell her to get a life? Obviously, she'd been too easy on the little creep lately. It had been too long since she'd made Heathen scream for mercy. All she had to do was walk back through that door . . .

No, it wouldn't last long enough to be worth it, she thought reluctantly. Tomorrow night was the first football game of the season, and if she started something with Heather, her parents would ground her for sure. She'd miss seeing Jesse play in his season debut. After one last, longing look at the bathroom door, Nicole flopped onto her bed with the latest *New Image* magazine.

The photographs were familiar, soothing, but Nicole barely saw them. As much as it killed her to admit it, Heather's comments had hit home. Was it possible—was there any chance at all—that she was as vain and shallow as Heather said?

Be serious, Nicole. Heather's just a stupid eighth-grader. She wouldn't know a life if she saw one. Nicole flipped the magazine pages slowly, studying the models. These women *all* had lives, and they had them because they were thin. Thin and beautiful. *That's how you get what you want in this world— everyone knows that.*

Everyone except that idiot Heather.

Eight

"I don't want to sit in the front row," Courtney whined as she followed Nicole down the bleachers. "Only geeks sit in the front."

"Only geeks and us," Nicole muttered under her breath.

The Friday-night football game was about to begin, and it seemed as if the whole town had turned out to watch. The noise was already deafening and the Wildcats hadn't even kicked off yet. All around them students crowded the stands, laughing, talking, and shouting across the rows to each other, while the adults and little kids took seats higher up, out of the chaos. Nicole reached the wide concrete walkway at the bottom of the bleachers and turned right, her eyes still on the space she hoped to squeeze into.

"Are these seats saved?" she asked a girl with black hair.

"No, go ahead."

Nicole and Courtney took their places—Nicole relieved that they'd managed to get a good view of the field, and Courtney annoyed by where it was. It was true that the coolest section to sit in started about ten rows back at the fifty-yard line, but there wasn't a whisper of a gap left there, and that was Courtney's fault for being so late getting ready.

"So what do you think?" she'd asked, when she finally showed up at Nicole's front door. She'd turned a slow circle on the doorstep so that Nicole could admire her from every angle. "I would have been on time, but I had to redo my hair."

Nicole had grimaced nervously. "I think we'd better get out of here before my parents see you. Bye, Mom! Bye, Dad!" And they'd hurried out to the car, Courtney laughing all the way.

"Your parents are so conservative—I don't know how you stand it. My parents said I look *great*."

Nicole glanced at her friend now as they waited for the game to start. She *did* look great. She was wearing a white eyelet bustier under an open black leather jacket, with black jeans and chunky black boots. The black clothing made Courtney's hair seem the color of fire, and she'd curled it and pinned it up in such a way that a mass of wild red ringlets tumbled down her back. Nicole felt invisible by comparison, even though she'd taken plenty of time on her own hair and outfit.

Courtney saw Nicole looking at her and inclined her head to whisper in her ear. "You have to admit, we add a lot of class to this section of the bleachers."

Nicole smiled, admiring Courtney's confidence.

"Don't forget," Courtney added. "The Spring Fling dress. I'm thinking I'll pick it up tomorrow."

So that was what Courtney was up to—working on winning that stupid bet. Nicole glanced at her friend one last time, noticing the way the black liner around her eyes made them seem twice as green. *Oh well, I never really liked that dress anyway.* But then an unexpected second thought brought a smile to Nicole's thin lips. *Besides, I'd like to see her try to zip it.*

"Something funny?" Courtney asked.

"I doubt you'd think so."

"Hey, Nicole! Nicole! Hi!" someone called down suddenly from a few rows back. Nicole turned around to see Jenna waving wildly, with Peter at her side. "I thought that was you!" Jenna shouted. "Isn't this fun? I'm so excited."

"Yeah. Hi." Nicole waved back self-consciously, hyperaware of Courtney's presence at her side. She could imagine what her friend must be thinking: *It's bad enough we had to sit in the loser section, Nicole, but do you have to admit that you know its inhabitants? Not cool, Nicole. Not cool at all.* "Well, uh, see you guys later."

Peter and Jenna waved good-bye and Nicole turned back around in her seat.

"Do you know those people?" Courtney demanded immediately.

"Kind of. We worked together at the carnival."

"Well, I'd deny that if I were you. I had that pair in English lit last year, and between them they found Jesus in every book we read. The God Squad, I called them. Every time an author came anywhere *near* to alluding to the Bible, those two got excited."

"That's hardly a crime, Courtney."

Courtney raised one thinly plucked eyebrow.

"I mean, Jenna and Peter are okay," Nicole added lamely. "They worked really hard at the carnival."

"Well, of course they did. Isn't that part of the package? Love your brother and do unto others and all that?"

"You make it sound like a bad thing." Nicole hated discussing religion with Courtney. "Can't we change the subject?"

"I don't think it's a bad thing at all. I just don't see why the world needs to make up gods to tell it what to do. Can't people help each other out of the kindness of their hearts?"

"Oh, like *you*, you mean. You were a *big* help."

Courtney stared, visibly amazed by Nicole's sarcasm. A second later, though, her expression settled into a vaguely embarrassed smile. "Touché."

Then the cheerleaders ran out onto the brightly lit field and the bleachers erupted into raucous, spontaneous cheering. Nicole dropped her discussion with Courtney gratefully, focusing instead on

Melanie sprinting over the grass behind Tanya Jeffries. The cheerleaders were nearly halfway to the fifty-yard line when the Wildcats burst out of the tunnel behind them and the noise got even louder. Nicole immediately forgot all about Melanie as her eyes combed the players for Jesse.

"*I know who you're looking for,*" Courtney teased in a singsong voice.

"Will you give me a five-second break? Why don't you go hit on some poor guy or something?"

Courtney simply laughed. "First I have to pick one."

"*Go, Wildcats!*" Melanie shouted, her right fist extended into the air, her left fist on her hip. Each of her size-six Nikes was planted firmly on the back of a fellow cheerleader, and those two girls were kneeling on the backs of three others.

"Go, Wildcats!" the crowd thundered back.

Holding her breath with mixed fear and excitement, Melanie leaned out until she fell blindly back toward earth. This was her favorite part of the spirit pyramid: falling backward, out of control, knowing that if Tanya and Lou Anne didn't catch her she could be badly hurt. Knowing they'd catch her, Melanie hit the cradle of their arms right on target and was tossed forward onto her feet.

The crowd cheered and Melanie became aware of her heart beginning to beat again, of the blood pumping through her body. She was alive, and she threw a spontaneous back handspring to prove it. Nothing she knew compared to the thrill she got from a dangerous stunt.

"Go, Wildcats!" the entire squad shouted again, in perfect unison.

It was the signal for the players to come back out from the halftime break, and they ran onto the field immediately, causing pandemonium in the stands. The cheerleaders held a line at the edge of the field as the guys swarmed around them, some heading for the field and some the bench, all of them shouting with pent-up excitement.

Then Kurt Englbehrt jogged out beside Coach Davis, the smile on his face incandescent. Even though he wasn't playing, he was obviously thrilled simply to be with the team again. The crowd caught sight of him in his jeans and Wildcats jersey and roared even more loudly. The cheers and stomping in the stands were so prolonged that Coach Davis finally sent Kurt into the middle of the field to take a bow. Kurt trotted out jubilantly and doffed his baseball cap to the fans, exposing the bald head that was no longer a symbol of his sickness but a reminder of his recovery.

Melanie felt happy tears burning her eyes. Kurt's cancer was really gone, and in her own small way she had helped make that happen. It felt incredible. A moment later, Kurt ran back off the grass and the players scrambled for their positions.

"We're killing them!" rejoiced a sudden voice in Melanie's ear, catching her off guard. A rough hand slapped her behind.

Melanie wheeled to face Jesse, furious. He wasn't even supposed to be talking to her, let alone mauling her in front of the entire school. All the joy of the moment before vanished in intense irritation.

"Maybe you get away with that crap with your little boyfriends," she told him, her eyes narrowing to slits. "But if you touch me again, I'll deck you."

Jesse laughed. His cheeks were ruddy with exercise and excitement, and his eyes had a wild, transported expression about them. "Ooh. You'd better calm down, hot stuff," he teased. "I might just take you up on that."

"I mean it, Jesse! Get away from me." She turned her back on him.

"You know, you're even sexier when you're angry," he said, his voice a teasing whisper. Then he ran off down the field.

Melanie could feel the blood invading her cheeks as she stood facing the stands. She wondered how many people in the audience had noticed what Jesse had done, and how it must have looked to them. *Stupid Jesse,* she thought, taking some deep, deep breaths. One of these days that guy was going to force her to put him in his place.

At last the cheerleaders began leaving the field, marching single-file toward the bleachers. Melanie was able to make out faces in the audience easily as the crowd got increasingly closer. Then, right in the front row, she noticed Nicole staring at her. Melanie raised one hand slightly in acknowledgment, even though she wasn't supposed to. Instead of waving back, though, Nicole looked quickly away.

That's weird, Melanie thought as the cheerleaders marched on by. *I wonder what's up with her?*

"Okay, this is the final play!" Hank Lundgreen hollered, rallying his team around him. "Let's put this baby to bed!"

Jesse pushed forward in the huddle to hear Hank call the pattern. The Wildcats were murdering the Muskrats, and now the clock had all but run out. One last play and there'd be nothing left but the partying.

"Let's go!" Hank bellowed, breaking the huddle.

The teams took up positions, the ball was hiked, and Jesse charged off the line. All around him bodies collided, and the racket of crashing pads and helmets assaulted his ears even as the scents of sweat, mud, and turf attacked his nostrils. Jesse juked to the left, then ran right, faking his defender practically out of his cleats. He pushed past the other boy and flew down the sideline, an open receiver.

Jesse's legs pumped beneath him, his lungs sucked in the cool night air, and his arms swung easily at his sides—he felt it all with a sense of awed detachment. His body was clicking along like a machine, effortlessly doing whatever he asked it to. He reached open field and glanced back over his shoulder in time to see the football hurtling in his direction. It was a wild throw—too high and way to the left. Without hesitation, Jesse gathered himself and leapt, his legs launching him into space as his arms stretched out in front of him: reaching, reaching . . .

The pebbled surface of the ball smacked his palms, and Jesse quickly trapped it against his chest. Only then did he notice that he was several feet up in the air—and coming down facefirst. He ducked his head and held on, his entire concentration focused on not fumbling. The buzzer went off. The ground struck him hard behind his left shoulder. Jesse rolled forward onto his feet and sprang up, unhurt, holding the ball triumphantly skyward in one strong hand.

"Yeah!" he yelled, spiking the ball. "Yes!"

He turned to the stands, his arms thrown open wide, and the crowd didn't disappoint him. They screamed their approval, their adoration. What a game he'd had, and what a way to end it!

Then the rest of the team caught up with him. The next thing he knew, he was buried under an avalanche of flesh and clattering equipment. "Way to go!" his teammates yelled, beating on his helmet, his pads, whatever they could reach. "Jones! You stud! Way to go!"

He hadn't gotten the touchdown, but it didn't matter. The game had been won well before the last play anyhow—Jesse's spectacular catch had simply added the exclamation point. Coach Davis blew his whistle and the dogpile finally struggled back onto its feet.

"Good game, everyone," he congratulated them, his voice just a wheeze from shouting throughout the game. "Jones, way to hustle!"

Jesse beamed at his coach's praise, knowing he'd never played better. As the team trotted off to the locker room, he couldn't erase the smile from his face. CCHS had a great team—a great chance at the title. And now Kurt was back with them, in spirit, anyway. Maybe he'd even be able to play again by the time the Wildcats reached the championships.

Joy welled up inside him until Jesse laughed out loud. What a fool he'd been to think something was missing in his life. All he'd needed was for football to start again!

"It says here that there's a football game at the high school tonight. Why didn't you go, Leah?" Mr.

Rosenthal put down his newspaper and looked at her expectantly.

Leah laughed. "Please, Dad. I've made it all the way to senior year without seeing one. I'm trying to graduate with my record intact."

"I never liked football either," Leah's mother said.

The three of them were lingering around the small dining room table after a late dinner, sipping the strong, black coffee her parents preferred and sharing sections of the newspaper.

"I don't know if I *dislike* it. It just seems kind of pointless, that's all," Leah clarified. "I mean, even if you win, what have you really accomplished? Who even remembers the score after a day or two goes by?"

Mr. Rosenthal chuckled. "You mean, besides the team, the coach, and at least half of Clearwater Crossing? The Wildcats have a chance at the title this year, you know."

Leah shrugged, unimpressed. "Maybe I'll go to one of our water polo matches."

"Water polo! Now *there's* an exciting sport," her father teased.

"What in the world has you interested in water polo?" asked Mrs. Rosenthal. Leah's parents were used to her coming up with new and unusual interests at least a couple of times per month, but even Leah had to admit that water polo was pretty far outside her normal tastes.

"One of the guys I worked with at the carnival is on the water polo team. Maybe I'll go watch him play sometime."

"Water polo," Mr. Rosenthal repeated, shaking his head in disbelief. "What's this boy's name?"

"Miguel del Rios. He's in my biology class, too."

An amused smile crept over her father's features. "How *is* biology, anyway? Have you given your teacher any new heart attacks lately?"

"No," Leah answered with a giggle. "I'm giving her the rest of the semester off for good behavior."

Leah had told her mother and father all about the Darwinian disaster the day it happened. She told her parents just about everything. She loved that they were so intelligent and open-minded. Even when they didn't take her side, they always listened and gave her a fair chance to explain. It was great being an only child with parents like hers.

"It must seem strange going to school without Daryl this year," Mrs. Rosenthal said, changing the subject. "Are you making other friends?"

Leah shrugged. "Sure. But no one like Daryl. It's not like I'm going to replace her or anything." Daryl Holiday had been Leah's best friend since junior high. When Daryl's family had unexpectedly moved to Chicago during the summer, Leah had been crushed.

"The two of you were so close—never doing anything with anyone else. I always worried about what would happen to you if something ended that friendship."

Leah smiled. "I'm not exactly *lost* without her, Mom. I do know a few other people. Besides, it's only for a year. Daryl and I are going to apply to all the same colleges."

"Starting with Clearwater University, I hope," her father said, winking at his wife.

"Oh, sure. Like I really want to go to a school where the entire faculty knows my parents. No, I'm thinking Stanford—outstanding academics, California sunshine, and total anonymity."

Mr. Rosenthal clutched theatrically first at his heart, then at his wallet.

Mrs. Rosenthal smiled. "You didn't really want to retire before you were ninety, anyway, did you, dear?" she teased.

Nine

Melanie pumped hard at the pedals of her dad's old bicycle, enjoying the way the warm September air made her hair stream out behind her. The party after the Wildcats' win the night before had gone on forever, and she'd spent most of the morning sleeping it off. It hadn't even been much fun—just a lot of conceited guys bragging about how great they were and a lot of delusional girls sucking up to them. Melanie had hoped that Kurt and Dana might show up, but they hadn't. Hank had finally told her that Kurt still needed to take it easy. By the time Melanie had left, her head pounding and her clothes reeking of cigarette smoke, she'd already known she wouldn't be going to the party the Wildcats were throwing on Saturday. Tonight.

Melanie rode the bike toward town, planning to cruise through the park. Most of the stores hadn't opened yet, and the streets were all but deserted. Reaching the park at last, Melanie hopped the curb from Clearwater Boulevard. The cranky old bicycle rattled and bucked beneath her as she cut across the grass, then popped up onto one of two wide concrete paths bisecting the park.

Clearwater Crossing Park was large and old, with huge shade trees providing welcome relief from the sun in the summer months. Picnic benches and stationary barbecue grills clustered under the trees, with lush stretches of grass in between. At the far end of the park, out of sight, were playing fields and a lake, which was occasionally stocked with bass for junior anglers. Melanie guided her bike along the path she was on, heading toward the center of the park. Up ahead, where the two main paths intersected, Melanie could see the little cluster of park buildings: the office, the activities center, and the rest rooms.

As Melanie coasted in closer, she noticed about fifteen little kids gathered outside the activities center. A couple of large artist's easels had been set up, and the children were apparently there to paint, although the white butcher paper that flapped from the easels was still unmarked. The kids stood around with dry paintbrushes in their hands, looking impatient, and Melanie slowed her bike curiously. *What are they doing?* she wondered. *Where are the adults?*

Melanie stopped on the path about thirty feet away, reminded of happier times when she used to paint with her mother. A few seconds later, though, her thoughts were interrupted when four of the boys began an impromptu sword fight with their paintbrushes. They battled fiercely to the disapproving shrieks of the girls, who yelled at them to stop.

"Peter!" one of the girls cried out. "Jason broke his paintbrush!"

To Melanie's amazement, Peter Altmann walked through the open door of the activities center, a splash of dark green paint on the front of his white T-shirt. "Jason, man, we don't have the money to replace broken equipment. You shouldn't fight with the brushes."

Peter's tone was kind but harried, and Melanie smiled as she realized he must have been watching the whole thing through the windows.

"We're bored! We want to paint!" Jason retorted, not the least bit repentant. "You said we were going to paint, Peter."

"Yeah, Peter," echoed a chorus of young voices. "You said! You said!" The chorus became a chant. "We want to paint. . . . We want to paint. . . . *We want to paint!*"

"Okay, okay." Peter held up a hand for peace. "And you will. You just have to give me a couple more minutes to mix up the colors. Anyway, you guys haven't even put your smocks on yet—you're not *ready* to paint."

"I'm not wearing that nasty old smock," a tiny blonde with Shirley Temple ringlets announced. "It's covered with old paint."

"And you will be too, Lisa, if you don't put it on. That's what smocks are for."

"It looks like you should have taken your own advice," Melanie couldn't resist calling from the path.

Peter looked over, startled, then grinned. "Hi, Melanie."

"I keep running into you everywhere."

Peter put up his hands as if surrendering. "You're not going to run into me today, I hope. I can take you on foot, but the bike could make things more challenging."

Melanie groaned as she realized she'd set herself up. "Very funny. Anyway, I think you're already challenged enough." She nodded significantly at the group of milling kids, then pointed to his paint-covered shirt.

"I'm no artist," he admitted ruefully. "My friend Chris was supposed to help me, but something came up and he's going to be late."

"Peter!" a brown-haired girl whined, pulling down hard on one of his hands. "We want to paint!"

"No, we don't!" Jason cried. "We want to fight!"

With amazing speed, the little troublemaker snatched another girl's paintbrush away from her and attacked his sword-fighting buddies again. The girl whose paintbrush had been stolen began to cry, and a couple of her friends rushed into the fray, slapping at the fighters.

137

"Give it back!" a tall, skinny tomboy ordered. "You give that back right now!"

"Let's see you take it, Godzilla," one of the boys taunted.

"You take that back or I'll make you!" the tomboy shouted angrily. She grabbed her antagonist and started applying an Indian burn to the bare skin of his forearm.

"Okay! Break it up!" Peter waded into the middle of the altercation, separating the scuffling kids with ease. "Priscilla, no Indian burns—you know that. Danny, apologize to Priscilla for calling her a name."

"Sorry," Danny mumbled, his eyes on the dirt.

Priscilla tossed her short dark hair.

"Good. Now, Jason, give Amy back her paintbrush."

"Ah, *man!*" Jason whined, but he did it anyway.

Melanie watched the commotion with a mixture of amusement and admiration. *Peter might not know anything about painting,* she thought, *but he knows what he's doing with those kids.* Even from a distance it was clear how much they looked up to him.

"Okay," Peter told the group. "I'm sorry it's taking so long, but if you want to paint *today*, you need to settle down and help me out a little. I need a few more minutes to set things up, and that means a few more minutes *without* any fighting. Okay? Do you think you can do that?"

"Yes," a few of the kids answered. The sword-fighters hung their heads.

"Good. I'm counting on you guys." Peter started walking back toward the door of the activities center, but halfway there he seemed to remember Melanie, still up on the path on her bicycle.

"They're really nice kids," he called to her. "They're just a little restless today. I wish I could stay to talk, but I'd better try to get this show on the road."

"Is that tempera paint?" Melanie asked, pointing to his shirt again.

Peter shrugged. "Beats me. It's some kind of horrible powder that allegedly mixes with water."

"You ought to rinse it out before it dries. It might come out if you do it now."

"Do you think so?" Peter asked hopefully. "Jenna made me this shirt. See?" He pointed to some hand-embroidered lettering over the pocket, and Melanie squinted to read it. *Peter, Junior Explorers, Staff,* the colored thread spelled out in three lines of block letters.

Melanie swung off her dad's bicycle and stood beside it on the concrete. "I'm not really doing anything today. I could . . . I mean, if you want . . ." She shrugged, suddenly at a loss. "I know how to mix paint."

"You do?" Peter said excitedly. "And you want to help? That's great! Come on."

The next thing she knew, she was pushing the bike off the path and over some dirt to the door of the activities center.

"Just bring it inside and lean it anywhere," Peter told her, hurrying toward the sink and counter at the closest end of the large open room. There were a number of folding, cafeteria-style tables and chairs set up in the space, with a small dais and podium at the far end. Melanie propped her bike up near the door and joined Peter at the sink.

"Yuck!" she exclaimed when she saw the mess he'd made. Spilled paint powder lay in drifts on the Formica counter, surrounding several open plastic containers. A recycled half-gallon paper milk carton full of mixed red paint stood dripping to one side, next to another containing a putrid-looking brown. In the sink were a thick green puddle and the torn remnants of another paper carton.

"It exploded when I tried to lift it out of the sink," Peter explained sheepishly.

"You shouldn't put so much paint in them, and you shouldn't mix it so thick." Melanie bent to retrieve a clean milk carton from the floor. "Do you have any scissors?"

Peter rummaged hurriedly through a drawer underneath the countertop and held out some teacher's scissors. Melanie trimmed the top off the milk carton, then cut the height down to about one-third. "They're sturdier like this," she explained.

"Besides, it's better to make a bunch of small containers than one big one. More people can use them that way."

"We only have two good easels," Peter said, handing Melanie another milk carton to trim. "None of the other ones stand up." He pointed to a pile of collapsed, ancient easels in the corner. "I'm afraid the Junior Explorers program isn't exactly rolling in dough."

Melanie smiled as she thinned Peter's red paint and poured it neatly into three perfectly trimmed containers. "Is that what you call this group, the Junior Explorers?"

"Yep." Peter picked up the scissors and began trimming more cartons the way Melanie had shown him, keeping one eye on the window. "Most of these kids are from single-parent families or are in foster care. All of them are poor. My friend Chris and I started this program to give them something fun to do on Saturdays, but it also gives their parents a chance to take care of adult things. You know, like shopping and chores."

"You thought of this by yourself?" Melanie asked, surprised that someone as young as Peter could start his own park program.

"Me and Chris Hobart. He's in college, but I know him from my church."

Melanie dragged Peter's second carton full of paint closer to the sink and peered at it suspiciously. "What color is this supposed to be? Don't ask me what it looks like."

Peter laughed good-naturedly. "Lisa said she needed brown and green because she wants to paint trees. Of course we don't *have* brown, so I tried to make it by mixing colors. No good, huh?"

"It needs a little help." Melanie shook in red paint powder, then green, stirring the mixture until it became a deep glossy brown. She poured it expertly into three clean containers.

"I get the feeling you've done this before."

Melanie shrugged. "I used to paint with my mother when I was a kid."

"With poster paints?"

"No, watercolors. Most of my poster-painting got done in kindergarten." She turned to Peter, who'd finished quite a few more milk-carton containers. "Why don't you go rinse that shirt out? I can handle this."

"Really?" he said gratefully. "Thanks, Melanie. I'll hurry. I'll just be right outside if you need me." He put down the scissors and walked out into the sunshine, where he was greeted by an enthusiastic chorus of shouts and cheers.

"Peter! Are we going to paint now?" Melanie heard a Junior Explorer yell.

"In two minutes," Peter promised. "My friend Melanie is mixing the paint."

Melanie kept an eye on him as he crossed to a

spigot, stripped off his shirt, and held it under the rushing water, trying to rinse out the paint.

"Ooh, Peter. You're so *white*!" one of the girls told him.

You're not kidding, Melanie thought with a grin, returning her attention to the sink. Peter's torso had all the robust color of a sterile cotton ball.

By the time Peter returned in his wet, wrinkled shirt, Melanie had five colors of paint ready. Not only that, but she'd set up three more easels. "How did you do that?" Peter cried, rushing forward to inspect them. "I thought they were broken!"

"They're not in great shape, but they ought to hold up. I took a few nuts off the others." Melanie gestured to the pieces of the three remaining easels on the floor.

"That's great! I'll take them outside."

Soon Peter had all five working easels lined up on the packed dirt outside the activities center. Melanie started carrying out containers of paint as the kids crowded around her.

"Who are you?" one of the little girls asked. "Are you Peter's girlfriend?"

Melanie laughed uneasily, her eyes darting toward Peter to see his reaction. "No, just a friend." She began setting the paint containers on the ledges at the bottoms of the easels.

"Don't be stupid, Cheryl," Priscilla butted in. "That Jenna chick is Peter's girlfriend."

"You all know I don't have a girlfriend," Peter said patiently, putting extra clothespins on the easels to hold the butcher paper flat. "Who wants to paint first?"

"I do. Me!" fifteen voices cried.

Peter grimaced. "Dumb question." He quickly pointed to five of the only six kids wearing smocks. "Okay, you five can go first because you put on your smocks. Lisa, I see you have your smock on too, but you can go in the next group, okay?"

Lisa nodded, her blond ringlets bobbing. Sidling up next to Peter, she slipped her small hand into his. "I'll be your girlfriend, Peter."

"No, me! Me!" several of the other girls clamored while the boys pretended to gag.

"Peter doesn't need any stupid girlfriend," Jason declared. "He'd rather hang out with us guys."

A sudden lump made Melanie's throat ache as the kids competed for Peter's attention, the long-awaited paints completely forgotten. Peter wrestled with them while both boys and girls attacked his legs, squealing with joy and trying to pull him to the ground. Melanie stood off to one side, as forgotten as the paints.

"What's going on out here?" a male voice boomed suddenly from behind her. "What's all this fooling around?"

The Junior Explorers stopped roughhousing, their heads swiveling in unison.

"Chris!" Priscilla screamed, letting go of Peter's still wet shirt and launching herself at the newcomer. "Chris, you're here!"

The wrestling broke out on two fronts now as half the kids abandoned Peter to attack their other counselor. Melanie backed out of the melee, watching from a safe distance.

That guy Chris is adorable, she couldn't help thinking, even though he was probably five or six years older than she was. He wore faded Levi's and cowboy boots, and the muscles in his back and shoulders were evident beneath his black T-shirt. Dark glasses and a spiky brown haircut gave him the air of a low-key rock star, or maybe an actor on one of those hip police dramas. The lower edge of a tattoo peeked out below his right shirt sleeve and, curious, Melanie wished she could see the rest of it.

"Okay! Enough! Uncle, uncle!" Chris cried. "You win!"

He and Peter both straightened up, shaking off the more persistent Explorers. "Enough," Peter echoed.

Then Chris noticed Melanie. "Hi," he said, walking in her direction and extending one hand with an incredibly handsome smile. "I'm Chris Hobart."

Melanie shook his hand as Peter rushed over to explain. "This is my friend Melanie. She helped me set up the easels and mix all this paint. It's a good thing, too, since *somebody* was late," Peter added. "How did that go, anyway?"

Chris dropped Melanie's hand and rolled his eyes. "Maura shouldn't even be allowed to drive until she learns a few things about cars. She was *completely* out of oil—she's lucky she didn't throw a rod."

"Maura is Chris's girlfriend," Peter told Melanie.

Chris nodded, an amused smile on his face. "Called me on her cell phone in a panic. Told me the car was making 'a funny noise.' Everything's fine now, though. No casualties."

Chris turned back toward the kids, who were crowding in around them. "I thought we were going to paint!" he shouted.

"*Yeah!*" The five kids Peter had chosen to paint first charged the easels, holding their brushes high and studying their butcher paper canvases with mad gleams in their eyes.

"Do you know how to paint, Chris?" Peter asked quietly.

"You mean so's anyone can tell what it is? Not a clue."

Peter turned to Melanie. "Maybe you should hang around awhile longer."

Melanie glanced undecidedly from Peter to Chris to the Junior Explorers crowding around the easels. Jason had already started: three bold red lines intersected near a violent splash of yellow. Melanie smiled—an abstract expressionist. "I'd like to," she said hesitantly. "I just don't . . ."

"*Please*, Melanie." A small hand tugged at the hem of her shorts, and Melanie looked down to see little Amy, her dirty cheeks tear-streaked from the incident with the paintbrush. "It's no fun with only guys all the time."

"Well . . . I . . . ," Melanie stammered, surprised. She *wanted* to stay, but she didn't know if she was still welcome now that Chris had arrived. She looked worriedly at Peter, then at Chris. Both of them nodded at her encouragingly. "I guess I could stay a little while."

Amy smiled and reached for Melanie's hand. Melanie took the small hand inexpertly in hers, feeling self-conscious, but also flattered.

Chris leaned over to whisper in her ear. "Amy lost her mother to an overdose last year, and now she and her father live alone. She could really use a woman to look up to."

The poor kid! Sympathetic tears welled up in Melanie's eyes. Her hand gripped Amy's more tightly, and she crouched down next to the little girl. "What do you want to paint, Amy? A pony? A castle?"

"Something pretty," said Amy.

Melanie smiled and pulled Amy closer. "You and

I are going to paint the prettiest picture in the whole wide world."

"You're going *down* tonight, girlfriend." Courtney turned on her most alluring smile as she scanned the crowded party, simultaneously adjusting the neckline of her tight blue dress. "Tonight's the night I win our bet."

"If you say so, Courtney." That ridiculous bet was the last thing on Nicole's mind right then. She pressed back tightly against the living room wall, anxious to keep her new shoes from getting stepped on.

Where is *he?* she asked herself for the fifteenth time. *He was supposed to be here!* Her eyes roamed the mob in Hank Lundgreen's house, looking for Jesse.

Hank's parents were out of town, and it seemed as if most of the school had shown up at the wild open party Hank was throwing. Kids crowded the darkened living room and den, danced on the back patio, and piled three deep on every available piece of furniture. The line for the downstairs bathroom already extended all the way into the kitchen, where the people waiting for a turn made themselves even more uncomfortable by drinking cupfuls of pinkish orange punch. Football players took turns pumping the keg and pumping up the volume on the Lundgreens' blasting stereo, serving as self-appointed hosts.

"Hey, ladies, how 'bout some punch?" a slurred voice shouted over the music. "Issa house specialty!"

Nicole and Courtney turned to see a very drunk Barry Stein thrusting two dripping paper cups at them.

"What's in it?" Courtney took a cup of the punch and held it to her nose, sniffing curiously.

"If I tell ya that, I'll hafta kill ya." Barry laughed and pushed the second cup of punch into Nicole's unresisting hands before staggering off through the crowd again.

"Is *he* ever plowed!" Nicole exclaimed.

"No kidding." Courtney brought the paper cup to her lips and sipped cautiously at the punch. "Not bad. I've had worse." She took several deep swallows. "Try it."

Nicole sipped from her own cup, shuddering as the strong, bitter taste of nearly straight alcohol exploded in her mouth. "*Where* have you had worse?"

"Mike Sweeny's party. That punch was terrible."

"We *carried* you out of Mike Sweeny's party."

"So then I know what I'm talking about." A mischievous sparkle lit Courtney's green eyes.

"I'm surprised you remember," muttered Nicole.

"Hey, does one of you girls want to dance?" Nicole didn't know the guy who had just walked up to them, but he was cute—tall, with straight jet black hair falling forward over almond-shaped eyes.

"I do!" Courtney said immediately. "Bye, Nicole." The knowing wink Courtney gave her as her new dance partner led her back toward the patio seemed to say she had their bet in the bag.

"Bye."

Nicole pressed against the wall with her cup of punch, feeling conspicuous without Courtney. She was the only person standing by herself. It was totally embarrassing, not to mention socially risky—the last thing she needed was to look like a wallflower. She drank a few swallows of punch, ignoring the burning sensation in her throat, and cast around for someone else to talk to.

Lou Anne Simmons and Angela Maldonado were waiting in line for the bathroom. Nicole knew who they were—she knew who all the cheerleaders were. It was *possible* they'd remember her from last year's tryouts. . . . *No*, she decided, looking away. *If they don't, I'll be totally humiliated*. She still had one more opportunity to try out for the squad—she didn't need to hurt her chances by annoying the junior members now. *If Melanie were here, that would be different. I could make up an excuse to talk to her if I had to*.

Where is Melanie, anyway? Nicole was pretty sure she'd already seen all the other cheerleaders there.

Melanie seemed to be the only one missing. Just as Jesse was the only . . .

Nicole drained off the rest of her punch in a single gulp as her mind fast-forwarded to a horrible conclusion. What if Jesse and Melanie were *together*, out on a date somewhere?

"More punch," she muttered, pushing off from the wall. She didn't really want any, but it gave her an excuse to move. She was halfway across the living room when Barry's voice bellowed over the music again.

"Jesse! Jesse, you're the *man*! C'mon in, bud."

Barry and a few other players rushed past her to greet Friday night's MVP at the door. Nicole's heart pounded wildly, but she maintained her course to the kitchen without looking back. She had no intention of letting Jesse know how happy she was to see him. No, tonight she'd be as cool as she'd been pushy the week before.

"S'what are ya drinkin'?" Barry shouted. "The beer tastes better, but the punch is quicker."

"Better make it the punch, then." Jesse's voice was much closer than Nicole had expected. He was already almost right behind her!

Panicking, Nicole hurried straight past the kitchen, through the tiny den, and out onto the darkened patio beyond. Her hands shook as she looked around for a place to put her empty cup. *Get a grip on yourself,* she thought nervously, watching the dancers without really seeing them. She knew she had to talk to Jesse and smooth things over if she could. But now that the chance was finally here, she was so terrified of blowing it that she could barely even think.

Nicole sidled slowly back over to the patio door and glanced in through the glass. From where she stood, she could see the den and most of one end of the kitchen. Jesse, Barry, and a few other guys stood around the punch bowl, drinking and laughing loudly. Nicole thought about going in, then changed her mind. She didn't want to talk to Jesse in front of his friends. Sooner or later the group would break up. She'd wait. Meanwhile, there was at least one piece of good news to cling to: Melanie Andrews was still nowhere to be seen.

"Hey, Nicole! Come and dance!" Courtney darted forward and grabbed Nicole by the wrist, pulling her into the crowd. Courtney's cheeks were flushed from dancing and her hair frizzed around her like a wild red cloud. She tugged Nicole along behind her, bouncing in time to the music.

"I'm not going to dance with you, Court," Nicole protested, embarrassed.

"Not with *me*, silly. With Jeff! Keep him company while I go find a bathroom." Courtney pushed her forward and Nicole found herself face-to-face with the guy they'd met in the living room.

"Uh, hi," she mumbled, glancing back over her shoulder as Courtney abandoned her again.

The music kicked in and they started to dance. Jeff turned out to be a good dancer, which Nicole appreciated since the two of them ended up dancing four songs together before Courtney finally reappeared.

"You would not believe the line for the bathroom!" she exclaimed. "In a few more minutes it's going to be all the way out the front door."

"I missed you," Jeff said, smiling flirtatiously.

Courtney beamed. "Did you tell Nicole we're going out next weekend?"

Nicole knew from Courtney's tone that her friend would be around to collect on their bet the next day.

Jeff looked confused. "I didn't know Nicole was coming."

"I'm not," Nicole said hastily. "Well, nice meeting you, Jeff. I'm going inside now." She hurried off the dance floor and into the house through the patio door. Jesse and his friends still surrounded the punch bowl and Nicole paused uncertainly in the den.

Jesse seemed to be telling some sort of story. The hand he held his punch cup with gestured wildly, slopping punch in all directions. "I couldn't believe the way Hank laid it up there—like I'm Michael Jordan or something!" His audience howled appreciatively, and Nicole realized they were reliving Jesse's final catch of the night before.

It was also pretty clear that Jesse was getting drunk. His cheeks were flushed, and his voice was loud and overanimated. If she waited much longer, talking to him tonight would be pointless. Taking a deep breath, Nicole started walking toward the kitchen.

"Nicole!" Jesse cried when he saw her. "Nicol-ey. What are you doing here?"

"I . . . I want some punch," she lied, astonished by the warmth of his reception. She grabbed a paper cup off the stack and got in line to fill it. *Be cool*, she reminded herself.

"*Punch?* I thought you'd come to visit *me*." Jesse's loud, disappointed voice carried over the music, causing people in the living room to stop and turn their heads.

"Nope. Sorry."

Nicole could feel her cheeks heating up, and her heart pounded excitedly. Jesse seemed really glad to see her! She stepped up to the counter and took her time ladling punch into her cup.

"Do you know the guys?" Jesse asked, waving toward his friends. "Guys, this is Nicole. Nicole, these are the guys."

Her cup full, Nicole turned to smile at them.

"Isn't she cute?" Jesse asked the room in general. "She follows me wherever I go."

"I do not!" Nicole protested, horrified, but before

154

she could say another word, Jesse grabbed her and pulled her into his arms.

"Yes, you do." And then he kissed her. Full on the mouth, right there in front of everyone.

Nicole couldn't believe it was happening. She resisted, her arms stiff at her sides, her right hand still gripping her cup. Jesse didn't seem to notice. His lips pressed hers insistently. *Why is he doing this?* she wondered frantically. But as the kiss lingered on, Nicole felt herself beginning to melt. After all, wasn't this exactly what she wanted?

She gave in, relaxing against him and opening her mouth to his. He tasted of alcohol, but so did she. She kissed him more boldly, her free arm wrapping around his neck. Then someone took the cup out of her hand and she encircled Jesse with that arm, too. Jesse pulled her closer and kissed her deeply, kissed her until she forgot they were standing in the middle of a crowd in someone else's brightly lit kitchen. Nicole's heart beat crazily and her legs sagged beneath her as she held on to Jesse, kissing him for all she was worth.

Ten

"Do you want me to go slower?" Peter called over his shoulder. His voice carried back to Jenna on the mild afternoon air, filtering through the shimmering dust and the first dropping leaves of fall.

Jenna laughed. "Please! I could take you at any moment." She put more legwork into pumping her bicycle, as if to prove her point. The distance between them closed a little.

"Right. I forgot," Peter said, smiling. He slowed down anyway.

Jenna pedaled along behind him, happy to be with her best friend on such a beautiful Sunday. Her long hair streamed out behind her as she rode, and the fall sunshine warmed her shoulders through her shirt. The mountain bikes bounced and rattled along the gravel trail, passing fields of long dry grass and enormous hardwood trees. Up ahead, Jenna saw their favorite tree and the old tire swing dangling from one of its wide, spreading branches. She stood up on her pedals in a burst of renewed energy.

"Race you!" she called as she drew even with Peter, then shot by him.

"Hey! No fair!"

Jenna could hear Peter laboring to catch up, but she had the lead now. She wove erratically back and forth on the path to prevent him from passing.

"You're cheating!" Peter protested.

"You're right." Jenna laughed. "How else am I going to win?"

The path opened out into a large circle of packed bare dirt near the base of the tree, and Jenna couldn't block Peter's way anymore. He passed her easily and shot forward to the tree trunk, tagging it first while still on his bike. "Hah!" he gloated. "If you'd played fair, I might have let you beat me."

Jenna pulled up beside him and climbed off her bicycle, leaning it against the tree. She stretched lazily, a mischievous smile on her face. "You *always* let me beat you. I wanted to do it myself this time."

Peter grinned. "Keep trying." He swung off his bicycle and leaned it up against Jenna's, then shrugged his backpack off his shoulders.

"Did you bring any cookies?" Jenna asked hopefully.

"Of course. Where's the blanket?"

Jenna unhooked the bungee cord that held the tightly rolled picnic blanket to the rack on the back of her bike. Then, walking around to the other side of the tree, she unrolled the old plaid blanket with a shake and spread it out on the bare ground near the trunk. Jenna and Peter dropped happily onto the blanket, as they had a hundred times before, the sloping grassy field spread out at their feet.

"I brought grapes, too," Peter said, unzipping his pack and pulling out a steamy plastic bag.

Jenna made a face. "Sounds healthy. What kind of cookies did you bring?"

Peter put the grapes on the blanket, then brought out a couple of submarine sandwiches, two juice boxes, a big bag of corn chips, and finally a package full of Oreos.

"Ooh, good choice!" Jenna said approvingly. She and Peter traded off bringing the food for their picnics and they always had something good, but Jenna was never one hundred percent certain that Peter would come through in the dessert department.

"What were you and Chris talking about after church today?" Jenna asked, ripping into the chips.

Peter groaned. "Junior Explorers. Chris found out last night that the city funding for our replacement bus fell through."

"You're kidding! How could it?"

"Budget problems." Peter shrugged. "I don't know."

"But they can't do that!" Jenna exclaimed, outraged. "Don't they know those kids are counting on that bus?"

Peter smiled ruefully. "Maybe we should send you down to the next council meeting to explain it to them."

"Oh, I'll explain it to them, all right!" Jenna was getting more fired up by the minute at the thought of such unfairness. "We ought to *all* go down there and explain it to them."

The Junior Explorers had been given a decrepit old school bus when the program had first started, but the bus had barely limped through the summer and had died with a bang at the end of August. The bus allowed the kids to go on field trips and to summer camp—to do all kinds of fun things they couldn't afford if they had to pay for transportation.

"I don't think it would do any good," Peter said. "Chris said the money's just not there."

"But they *promised* you the money. And the old bus was already junked."

"I know." Peter sighed unhappily and stared blindly at the horizon. "The kids are going to be so bummed."

"You aren't going to *tell* them!" Jenna said. "It'll break their hearts if they don't get to go to camp this summer."

For the last two years, Peter and Chris had run a free two-week summer camp for the Explorers at a church retreat upstate, on the Mississippi River. Jenna had helped out as an assistant counselor both years, along with Chris's girlfriend, Maura.

"What else am I going to do, Jenna? I can't exactly buy them a new bus out of my allowance. I wish I could."

"I don't know." Jenna sipped her apple juice. "But don't tell them yet, okay? I'm sure the money will be found somehow."

"And how, exactly, do you know that?"

"Because it'll be too awful if it isn't. You'll get that bus—wait and see."

"I wish I felt so optimistic."

"Wait and see," Jenna repeated confidently.

Peter pushed aside his uneaten lunch and stretched out on his back, crossing his hands behind his head. "You know who stopped by the park yesterday and helped us paint? Melanie Andrews."

"Melanie?" Somehow Jenna couldn't quite form the mental picture of sophisticated Melanie Andrews making dripping stick figures with a bunch of little kids. "What was she doing there?"

"I don't know." Peter's eyes gazed up at the canopy of leaves over their heads and the old, frayed rope of the tire swing, which twisted slightly in the breeze. "She was just riding her bike through the park, I guess, and she saw me making a mess of things. She's a really good painter. She and Amy painted this whole big ocean scene with palm trees and waves and little sand castles."

"Has Amy ever even *seen* the ocean?" Jenna asked. She didn't want to admit it, but the idea of Melanie helping out with the Junior Explorers kind of bothered her. If Peter had needed help, why hadn't he called *her*?

"I don't think either of them has. But that doesn't really matter, does it? Melanie told the kids that when you're painting, what you see in your head is more important than what you see in front of you."

"I guess."

"You know, Melanie is an interesting girl," Peter said, sitting up with a faraway look in his eyes.

Jenna absorbed it with horror. "Oh, please! Not you too!" she cried. "Tell me I didn't just hear you say that."

Peter turned to her, obviously taken aback. "What's the matter with you? I thought you liked Melanie."

"I do. It's just . . . well . . . it was nice to know one last member of the male species who didn't live and breathe for Melanie Andrews, that's all."

"You can't be serious!" Peter's astonished laughter rang out across the empty field. "Me and Melanie Andrews? Yeah, that'll happen." The mere thought seemed to crack him up. He laughed and laughed until Jenna felt foolish for jumping to conclusions.

161

"Oh. Wow," he said, when he could speak normally again. "That wasn't what I meant at all."

"Then what *did* you mean?"

Peter's eyes became distant again. "I mean, she's different. You should have seen her with the kids. . . ." He trailed off, remembering. "I think she's lonely."

"Lonely!" Now it was Jenna's turn to laugh. "Melanie Andrews? You're nuts."

Peter smiled. "Maybe. But I don't think so. There's something about her . . ."

"Well, *I* never noticed it," Jenna said decisively. "And the next time you need help with the Junior Explorers, I wish you'd call me instead. Melanie has all the friends she needs without taking one of mine."

Peter made a face. "You know you're my best friend, Jenna."

Jenna smiled, satisfied. "Then how about proving it by pushing me on the tire swing?"

"What a party this weekend, huh?" Gary said. "You two were totally smashed." He pointed a finger at Jesse, then at Barry.

"Don't remind me," Barry groaned, squinting into the sunlight. "If I even think about it, I'll start hurling again."

Jesse could sympathize. He'd spent all day Sunday suffering through the most wicked hangover

162

imaginable, and Saturday night wasn't exactly a happy memory. Still, it wouldn't do to have his teammates think he was weak, and there were eight of them crowded around the outdoor lunch table that Monday.

"Come on, Barry," Jesse said, slapping his friend on the back. "You know what's good for a hangover? You get a can of creamed corn and put some in a shot glass. Then you break a raw egg over the top, toss it back, and gargle with it. Works every time."

Barry turned green and the other guys laughed.

"Probably because it makes you puke up anything even resembling alcohol," someone at the table guessed.

Jesse nodded sagely. He'd just made the whole thing up, but they didn't need to know that. "Where's Kurt?" he asked to change the subject. "I knew he wasn't coming to the parties, but I thought he'd be at school today."

"He's here. He and Dana went off campus for lunch," Dennis Peterson told him. "She's cooking him a special 'remission dinner' or something tonight and they're acting totally lovey-dovey. It's nauseating." The big tackle hunched his broad shoulders and shook his head disgustedly. "If that's what almost dying does for you, then I don't want to try it."

"Speaking of lovey-dovey," Barry said, a slightly

vengeful smile on his face, "guess who's on her way over here, Jesse? It's your old friend Hot Lips."

Jesse glanced up just in time to see Nicole bearing down on their table, dressed like even more of a fashion victim than usual. The smitten way she smiled when she caught his eye confirmed his darkest fear.

"Oh, great," he groaned, averting his gaze. "She thinks we're some kind of item now."

"What did you expect?" Barry said, smirking. "The two of you made a pretty big scene."

"I was drunk," Jesse countered. "Cut me some slack."

He remembered kissing Nicole at the party, barely—but ever since Sunday morning he'd been clinging to the slender hope that somehow *she'd* forget. The fact was, he wasn't even sure now why he'd done it. He remembered grabbing her in the kitchen and then, vaguely, making out on the patio, but after that it was all pretty black. It was a mystery to him how he'd even gotten home.

"Hi, Jesse!" Nicole said brightly, reaching his table. "You remember Courtney, right?"

Jesse had an immensely dim recollection of spilling a beer on the redhead at Nicole's side. "Yeah. Maybe."

Nicole walked around behind him and put two possessive hands on his shoulders. "So how are you feeling today? All better?"

"Better than what?" Jesse asked irritably, wishing she'd go away. He shrugged his shoulders out from under her hands and twisted around to face her.

"Well . . . better than Saturday night," she said hesitantly, the first glimmer of uncertainty flickering in those big blue eyes. "You were pretty sick by the time your friends drove you home."

"I was?" This was a nightmare. She was humiliating him in front of half the team.

"Don't worry, though. My shoes cleaned up fine. You'd never even know."

"Know what?"

Nicole threw a surprised sideways glance at Courtney, then focused on Jesse again and rubbed her hands together nervously. "That you . . . *you* know . . . barfed on them."

Jesse's friends roared with laughter and Jesse winced. That was a part of the evening he *definitely* didn't remember. It was clear he'd never live it down now, though.

"Oh." He was regretting touching her more every second. He didn't even *like* her—what had he been thinking? "I guess I was pretty drunk."

Nicole let out a relieved little giggle. "Yeah, you were. But you were so cute when—"

"No, Nicole," he interrupted harshly. "Understand me, here. I was *drunk*." He stared her down without blinking, willing her to take the hint.

At first she seemed as clueless as ever. Then

suddenly the laughter left her eyes. "You mean . . . you don't . . . ?"

"That's right. It was just a party, okay?" A couple of the guys sniggered and Jesse shot them an irritated glance.

Nicole's expression was positively crushed. "But you said—"

"I was drunk!" Jesse practically shouted. "Do I need to draw you a map?"

Nicole shook her head rapidly, her eyes on the pavement as the Wildcats howled at her expense. Courtney shot him a look that could have melted glass, but Jesse didn't need Courtney to tell him he was a jerk. Nicole's stunned face said it all.

"Look, Nicole," he said, lowering his voice. "It was just one of those things. Nothing personal, okay?"

She nodded, still not looking at him. He started to reach for her hand, then changed his mind. *Should I say something else?* he wondered. *What else can I say?*

Jesse's thoughts were interrupted by the welcome sight of Melanie crossing the quad, her blond hair shining, her expression as cool as ice cream. Melanie Andrews hysterical over a one-night fling was the last thing Jesse could imagine—a complete impossibility. He cast one last glance at Nicole, then lurched to his feet, desperate to get away from her.

"I've got to go, Nicole, okay? I need to ask Melanie something."

He was off before she could answer, grabbing his backpack and not looking back. Talking to Melanie was only an excuse, of course, but one he was happy to take. Anything to end that awkward scene.

You broke that girl's heart, his guilty conscience nagged as he ran across the quad.

But a second later, Jesse laughed out loud. *Stop flattering yourself. Nicole's a party girl. She'll be after somebody else in a heartbeat.*

"Don't give him the satisfaction," Courtney urged, rubbing Nicole's heaving back. "He isn't worth it." The two friends were huddled in a corner of the girls' room, their faces to the wall.

"But he *kissed* me," Nicole sobbed. "In front of *everyone*. He said he *liked* me."

"I know. The guy's slime."

Nicole was too distraught even to agree as she cried into Courtney's shoulder. After her lunchtime encounter with Jesse, she'd managed to hold herself together as far as the nearest girls' bathroom, but then she'd collapsed into tears. Now it was well into fifth period and she still couldn't stop crying.

"I just . . ." *Really liked him,* Nicole thought, unable to complete the sentence out loud.

When Jesse had kissed her at the party, Nicole had known that the entire school would find out about it in less than twenty-four hours. At the time, she could barely wait. She'd sailed through Sunday on hope and adrenaline. Even Heather's juvenile insistence that they arrive at church early again couldn't get her down. The rosy glow of the morning light sifting through the stained-glass windows had suited Nicole's mood perfectly. She'd drifted through the service with a dreamy smile on her face, barely hearing a word. After lunch, Courtney had arrived to collect on their bet. Nicole had handed over her Spring Fling dress without the slightest regret, then spent the afternoon shopping with her friend, looking for the perfect new outfit to wear to school on Monday. Something Jesse would really like her in . . .

Nicole had never felt like more of a fool in her life. The whole school knew about her and Jesse, all right. They knew he'd humiliated, betrayed, and abandoned her. What an idiot she'd been to think she could ever compete with Melanie!

"I hate them," she sobbed into Courtney's sweater. "I hate them both!"

"Both?" Courtney echoed.

"Jesse and Melanie. *Especially* Melanie!"

"That seems a little harsh. I mean, I can understand why you'd want to kill Jesse, but Melanie didn't have anything to do with it."

"She had *everything* to do with it!" Nicole cried,

pushing away from her friend. "This is all Melanie Andrews's fault!"

"And that would be because . . ." Courtney let the sentence dangle.

"Because all Jesse can think about is her! At the party, when Melanie wasn't around, he liked me just fine. But let Melanie sashay through the quad just once and he's back on her trail like Sherlock Holmes. It makes me sick!"

Courtney shook her head. "You can't believe that Mel—"

"I don't care what I believe!" Nicole shouted, bursting into fresh tears. "I'll never speak to either one of them again as long as I live!"

Eleven

From the desk of Principal Kelly
(Teachers: Please read in homeroom.)

Dear students:

It is with deepest sadness I must announce that Kurt Englbehrt died in an automobile accident last night. He was alone, driving home from dinner at a friend's house, when he apparently lost control of the car.

I know how many of you came together to help Kurt through his illness, and none of us can explain why a tragedy like this happens. I do know that the entire community joins me in mourning the loss of a fine student, an excellent athlete, and an outstanding human being.

There will be a student memorial service in Kurt's honor on the football field tomorrow after school. In the meantime, if any of you want to talk about this, we'll have counselors on campus for the next few days.

Remember, Kurt will always live on in our hearts. I know if he were here, he'd want me to end this message the way I alway do:

Go, Wildcats.

Mrs. Wilson was crying openly by the time she finished reading the principal's memo. Her voice gave out completely on the final word, and her hands shook as they clutched the crumpled paper.

Jenna stared at her teacher, stunned, unable to believe what she was hearing. What Mrs. Wilson had just told them was impossible! Kurt couldn't be dead—he'd just gotten well!

And then the first sob broke the silence. Someone at the back of the room had started crying. The tears spread out like a shock wave, radiating from their center until they engulfed the class. A cold, painful lump seized Jenna's throat as her own eyes filled, then spilled over. *This is really happening,* she thought. *This is real.*

She turned instinctively toward Miguel, but Miguel's head was down on his desk, his face covered by his arms. "Miguel," she whispered, reaching across the aisle to touch his shoulder. "Miguel, are you okay?" He drew away without raising his head, refusing to even look at her. She knew then that he was crying—either that or putting every bit of strength he had into holding back the tears.

All around her the sobbing grew louder. Jenna saw one of her own tears splash down onto the pages of her geometry book. She wiped distractedly at her wet cheeks, her fingers numb, as unfeeling as if they belonged to someone else. Her body was grieving ahead of her brain. She still couldn't take it in . . . wouldn't take it in . . .

"Jenna," Cyn Girard whimpered to her left. "Jenna!"

Jenna turned to see Cyn, normally coolheaded, streaming tears and mascara. Jenna slipped out of her seat and crouched in the aisle between desks to put her arms around the other girl.

"I can't believe it," Cyn sobbed as Jenna tried to comfort her. "This is going to *kill* Dana. And his poor *family*!"

Jenna held on to Cyn while her own tears fell faster. It was starting to overtake her now—the horrible finality of what had happened. The numbness was giving way, and a deep, insistent ache was growing in its place. The two girls rocked back and forth together, trying to shake loose the pain.

"Why?" Cyn demanded suddenly. "Why did this happen?" She pushed away from Jenna, searching her face for an answer.

Jenna struggled to think what her father might say, or Reverend Thompson, but there were no words, no reason that made sense. She shook her head. "I don't know." Then she closed her eyes and prayed.

Dear God, please help us through this. Let Kurt be with you, and let Dana and his family be comforted. Please watch over us all, and help us to understand.

And help Cyn, especially, if I let her down just now. I wish I could have given her an answer, but I don't have one yet. Please be with us today and always, and grant us the faith to believe that things like this happen for a reason. In Jesus' name, amen.

"I . . . I just can't believe it," Nicole said numbly, looking to Courtney for solace. "How can he be dead?"

Courtney shrugged as traffic surged around them in the hall, full of hushed tones and tear-streaked faces. "These things happen."

"That's not much of an explanation," Nicole protested.

"Sorry. It's the only one I have."

Courtney seemed as bewildered as Nicole. They'd both cried off and on all through homeroom, and now Nicole felt drained, shell-shocked. She leaned back against her locker, desperate for Kurt's death to make sense. He was only seventeen—a year older than she was. How could he just . . . *die?*

"I can't believe it," she repeated.

"It *is* pretty perverse." Courtney sighed. "I mean, after everything the poor guy just got through, to have his number come up like *that* . . ."

Nicole shuddered. Only yesterday her entire world had been in tatters because Jesse Jones had snubbed her. Now she felt ashamed to remember the way she'd cried and carried on over something so insignificant. Kurt's death was a *real* tragedy. In comparison, her crisis of the day before was nothing more than the disappointed tantrum of a selfish little girl.

All summer long, in fact, and ever since school had started, Nicole had been so wrapped up in her own petty agenda that she'd barely spent a moment thinking of anyone else. Even the one worthwhile thing she'd done—working at Kurt's carnival—hadn't come out of any real desire to help. It had all been about her and Jesse. If only she *had* done it for Kurt! At least she'd have that memory to comfort her. . . .

And then Nicole remembered the day the week before when Heather had caught her crying on the bathroom scale. She could almost hear her sanctimonious little sister laughing at her again, calling her vain and self-centered, telling her she needed to get a life. . . .

Nicole's eyes widened as the unthinkable sank in. "Heather was *right!*" she gasped.

Leah spotted Miguel walking along the edge of the quad and hurried her steps. Almost since the moment she'd heard about Kurt's accident, all she'd been able to think about was Miguel. Maybe it was because Miguel had seemed so connected to Kurt at the carnival, or maybe it was because she'd run into Jenna earlier, who'd told her Miguel was upset. Whatever it was, Leah wanted desperately to talk to him, to make sure he was all right.

"Miguel!" she called, her long legs easily closing the distance between them. "Hey, Miguel, wait up!"

Miguel hesitated near the corner of the cafeteria, and Leah wove quickly through the lunchtime throng of students, happy that she'd found him.

"Hi," she said breathlessly, stopping a couple of feet away. "I've been looking all over for you."

Miguel's dark eyes were inscrutable. "What for?"

"Well, uh, I thought maybe we could get some lunch and sit down somewhere," she said, thrown off by his reaction.

"I'm not hungry," he growled.

After talking to Jenna, Leah had been prepared to find him crushed, withdrawn, or even in tears, but his surliness was a surprise. "Look, Miguel," she said soothingly. "What happened to Kurt is terrible. I know how upset you must be. I thought we could talk about it."

Miguel stood at the edge of the quad like a statue. Leah had the sudden, strange feeling that if she poked him she might break a fingernail. His unfocused eyes gazed up into space, as soft as new velvet, but when they finally came back down to hers, they were hard and lifeless—completely devoid of emotion.

"Kurt's dead." Miguel's voice was as flat as his eyes. "What is there to talk about?"

It was the last question Leah had expected. "What? Well, to be honest, I'm not sure I know anymore." All she'd wanted was to be a friend, to help him through a bad time. But, as usual, he was making everything hard. "Can't we please just sit down and have lunch together?"

"I'm not sure I'm staying for lunch."

"Fine, *don't* eat lunch with me," Leah retorted, exasperated. "In fact, excuse me for even suggesting it. I don't know why I bother with you." She turned on her heel and stalked away, determined to find a better use for her time.

"Leah, don't be mad," he called after her. "You don't understand."

"You're right, I *don't* understand!" Leah said angrily, wheeling around to face him again. "And I'm getting pretty sick of trying, too. It might shock you to hear this, but the fact that you're the 'great' Miguel del Rios means nothing to me. No—*less* than nothing, all right? I thought you wanted to be friends, but if you don't, that's fine too. Believe me, I'll survive either way." She stared him down, daring him to make an excuse.

"I . . . I'm just upset about Kurt," he muttered at last, averting his eyes.

"Well, no kidding. We *all* are. That's what I've

been trying to tell you! You don't have to go through this alone, Miguel. Why can't we talk about it?"

"I . . . No." He turned his head away, and Leah thought she saw the beginnings of tears beading in his lashes.

She hesitated, then took a tentative step forward and put a gentle hand on his forearm. "Listen, Miguel, I'm sorry. I know Kurt was your friend—I should have been more understanding. But if you don't want to talk to me, maybe you ought to talk to one of the grief counselors. That's what they're here for."

"I just *don't . . . want . . . to talk about it!*" he said through gritted teeth. Wiping roughly at his eyes, he turned around to face her again, jerking his arm from under her hand. The color had risen in his cheeks, flushing them a deep, angry red. "Talking is a waste of time."

"Miguel—"

"No! You want to talk about it, Leah? Okay, let's talk about it." His voice had risen to an ugly pitch—people on the quad turned to look. "Life's a *joke*, Leah. Did you find that in any of your world religions?"

She stared at him, stunned, unable to answer. He was furious, out of control.

"No! Because they don't *tell* you that, take it from me. They don't tell you how unfair life is, or how random or stupid. We're all just supposed to be good and hope for the best. It's an insult!" His voice was getting louder by the second. "Well, let me tell you something, Leah. The only thing you can count on in life is *dying*. Being good doesn't get you squat!"

A crowd was starting to gather. Leah stretched out her hand to quiet him, but Miguel stepped angrily out of her reach.

"You want some evidence? Take Kurt Englbehrt!" He stood glowering at her, seemingly ready to implode. For a moment she thought he was going to say more. Then, suddenly, he turned and sprinted off toward the student parking lot.

The crowd gradually drifted apart, but Leah remained frozen at the edge of the quad, flabbergasted. It was the longest speech she'd ever heard Miguel make—the longest speech by far—and she hadn't agreed with a single word he'd said.

It's over, she thought as she watched his broad back disappear. *Whatever it was between us, that was the end of it.*

She knew for certain now that she and Miguel del Rios had nothing in common at all.

The football players and cheerleaders crowded tightly into two long rows of cafeteria tables, talking about Kurt in solemn voices. Most of the cheerleaders were crying, or at least wiping their eyes, but not Melanie. She sat before her untouched tray, a completely blank expression on her face.

Melanie didn't need a mirror to know her features gave away nothing. Hadn't she spent the last two years perfecting that expression? But she'd never managed to get the same degree of control over her stomach. The dull, frozen ache she felt there kept rising into her throat, threatening to gag her.

"Hey, Melanie, aren't you going to eat your lunch?" Jesse asked. Melanie had wanted to sit by Tanya, but Jesse and his friends had insisted on squeezing in between them and now Tanya was at the other end of the table.

"I'm not hungry," she told him dully. "Help yourself."

"I'm not hungry either." Jesse shoved her tray down the table, where a few of his less affected teammates divided up the contents. "It sucks about Kurt, doesn't it?"

Melanie nodded, afraid to trust her voice. No one at school had ever seen her cry. No one ever would.

"It's just awful," Tiffany said, butting in. "And such a waste after we went to all that work!"

"How can you *say* that?" Angela accused tearfully, glancing up from a pile of wet Kleenex. "My God, Tiffany."

Tiffany tossed her head and looked put out. "Sor-ry!"

"Poor Dana," said Vanessa. "That's who *I* feel sorry for. Can you imagine? Having him die like that—driving home from her little dinner? She must feel so guilty."

"My dad said the car was totally destroyed," Nate Kilriley said importantly. Nate's father was on the local police force. "They had to winch it out of the ditch and the front end was all twisted up, blood all over the windshield—"

Angela let out a howl and fled the table.

"Geez, Nate," Jesse snapped fiercely. "You think you could maybe shut up?"

This isn't happening, Melanie told herself over and over, relying on the mantra that carried her through everything. *Don't think about it. It isn't real. It isn't happening.* She could feel the bile rising up in her throat. *You can cry when you get home. You can think about it later.*

"Who died and made you king, Jones?" Nate snarled back. "I'll say whatever I want."

"Oh yeah?" Jesse's reply was low and challenging.

Nate began to stand up.

"Knock it off, you two," Hank warned from down the table.

Nate hesitated, but Jesse rose defiantly to his feet. *This isn't happening. It isn't happening.*

"What's the matter, Kilriley?" Jesse taunted. "I thought you wanted to kick my butt."

Melanie turned her head, unable to watch. *This isn't real.* Then, at the other end of the cafeteria, she saw Peter and Jenna talking by the exit. Their expressions were subdued, but not grim. Upset, but not hysterical. At that moment, Melanie thought they looked like the two sanest people in the room.

"You'd better be careful what you wish for, Jones," Nate threatened. "I might just give it to you."

Jesse snorted. "Bring it on."

Barely aware she was moving, Melanie rose from the table and started walking toward Peter and Jenna. Behind her, Jesse called out her name, but Melanie kept going without looking back. She was already halfway there.

"Hey, *Melanie!* Where are you going?" Jesse yelled again. She knew her entire group was probably wondering the same thing, but she didn't care anymore.

I need to talk to Peter, she thought, without the least idea why. She quickened her steps.

And then something made Peter turn toward her. Their eyes caught and held, and Melanie began to run. She was still a few feet away when something clicked in Peter's expression—the confusion on his face cleared into understanding. He opened his long arms wide as Melanie vaulted the final few steps.

"Oh, Peter!" she cried, flinging herself into his embrace and sobbing as if her heart would break.

An awed hush fell in the cafeteria.

"That's okay," Peter soothed in the silence. He closed his arms around her, stroking her shuddering back. "You're okay now."

Twelve

Jenna edged closer to Peter on the lush green grass as the CCHS students crowded onto the football field for Kurt's memorial service. "I wonder if Melanie will come," she said in a low voice. "I felt so bad for her yesterday."

Peter nodded. "I guess Kurt's death hit her two ways. I didn't know her mother was killed in a car wreck."

"Me either. She always walks around here like she's got the whole world on a string." Jenna shook her head. "Who'd have guessed?"

"I did, in a way. I told you she was lonely, remember?"

"I do now," Jenna admitted, thinking back to Sunday's picnic.

"Hi, guys," interrupted a quiet voice at Jenna's elbow. "Can I stand with you?"

Jenna turned to see a very dejected Ben Pipkin.

"Hey, Ben," she said warmly. "We *want* you to stand with us."

"Really?" He brightened microscopically. "Man,

this whole thing is so depressing. I can't believe he's gone."

Peter nodded sadly. "It was a horrible accident."

"Yeah," Ben said slowly. "But it's not just that. I mean, even when he was sick, I don't think anyone ever believed that Kurt would actually *die*. How could he? He was only a teenager! And then the way he finally went . . . just driving like that . . . completely sober . . . It could have happened to any of us."

"I know." Ever since she'd heard the news the day before, in fact, Jenna had thought of little else. She felt now that she'd been skipping through life with blinders on, foolishly assuming she'd have plenty of time to do whatever she wanted. But Kurt's death had shocked her into acknowledging something she'd never wanted to think about before: teenagers *could* die. No one was immune—not even her. She was still thinking about that when Leah drifted over, her tall form casting a shadow across the grass.

"Hi," Leah said. "I'm glad someone I know showed up for this thing. I wanted to come, but it's hard to listen to something so sad by yourself."

Jenna nodded as she looked around at the thickening crowd, then toward the makeshift platform with its white bunting, podium, and folding chairs. In a strangely appropriate twist, the platform had been placed at the end of the football field, right underneath a goalpost. A few students from the AV department milled around on the platform, adjusting the microphones, but there was no sign of the Englbehrt family. "When are they supposed to get started?" she whispered to Peter.

Peter checked his watch. "Any minute. Have you seen Melanie today?" he asked Leah.

"No. But there's Nicole." Leah waved.

Nicole was standing by herself a short distance away. If Leah hadn't pointed her out, though, Jenna was sure she'd never have recognized her. Instead of one of her usual trendy outfits, Nicole wore faded jeans, a man's ragged T-shirt, and sunglasses so large they covered half her face. Even more amazing, her usually perfect blond hair hung in limp, greasy strands on cheeks devoid of color.

"Nicole!" Jenna called, gesturing for the other girl to come over. Nicole looked up from her battered tennis shoes and shuffled toward them in slow motion.

"Man, what happened to her?" Ben whispered. "She looks *bad*." Peter hurriedly hushed him.

"Hi, you guys," Nicole said. She slouched into their circle next to Leah, then turned her attention back to her feet.

"Are you okay?" Leah asked, obviously concerned.

Nicole shrugged. "This hasn't exactly been the best week of my life." Leah put a sympathetic arm around her shoulders and Nicole didn't shake it off.

"Hi, Peter," Melanie's quiet voice said suddenly

from Jenna's other side. "Hi, Jenna. Can I hang out with you guys?"

Melanie was wearing sunglasses too, but aside from that she looked as coolly immaculate as always. All the cheerleaders were wearing their uniforms, and the Wildcats were wearing their jerseys in tribute. It was almost as if the day before had never happened . . . except that Melanie Andrews was hanging around with them now instead of with her usual gang.

"Sure," said Peter. "But aren't you supposed to stay with the team?"

"I don't feel like it. Besides, what are they going to do to me?" The expression on Melanie's face seemed to say she'd like to see someone tell her where to stand.

"No, stay with us," Jenna put in quickly. "It seems right for us all to be together. After all, it was Kurt who brought us together the first time." She glanced sadly around the football field, remembering a happier occasion on that same grass.

"Yes," Peter agreed. "Only now we need Jesse and Miguel."

"I doubt Jesse will disappoint you," said Melanie. She had no sooner spoken than Jesse burst out of the crowd and hurried to her side.

"What are you doing over here? The team is all supposed to stand together."

Melanie shrugged. "So sue me. I'm not in the mood for fistfights today."

"I *knew* you were mad about that," Jesse said, his voice low and embarrassed. "Listen, Melanie, I wasn't going to fight with Nate, but the guy was being a total jerk."

"You, on the other hand, behaved like a prince," Melanie drawled sarcastically.

There was a muffled sob from Nicole.

"Could we please not argue?" Leah said, looking from Jesse to Melanie. "Nicole is upset, and you two aren't helping."

"Sorry," Melanie murmured. "Sorry, Nicole."

Jesse acted as if he'd just that second noticed the rest of the group. "Oh, uh, hi, . . . everyone." He shifted his weight from foot to foot, abruptly nervous for some reason. "I, um, didn't realize we were all back together."

"Except for Miguel," Ben noted.

"I wouldn't hold my breath," Leah said.

Jenna was surprised by her friend's bitter tone, but before she could ask a single question, the Englbehrt family filed out onto the dais, accompanied by Hank Lundgreen, Coach Davis, and Principal Kelly. They all took seats at the edge of the platform as somber music played through the loudspeakers.

Dana Fraser came out to the podium, looking shaken and frail in a plain black sheath and sunglasses. She adjusted the microphone with a shaking hand and stood gazing out over the enormous group on the grass. The music faded out gradually and the crowd became silent, but still Dana said nothing. Every time she opened her mouth to begin speaking, her throat clenched convulsively and she had to stop. It was painful to watch, and Jenna felt tears sting her own eyes at the sight of Dana's struggle.

"This isn't how it was supposed to happen," Dana managed at last, her voice barely above a whisper. "I figured if I ever stood up to make a speech to y'all about Kurt, it would be because he'd been elected homecoming king, or won a football scholarship, or at least kicked all your butts on the SATs."

There was a brief, supportive chuckle from the crowd.

"I can't say I know why Kurt . . . died. And it's doubly hard when we were all so excited about the future. . . ." Dana paused to collect herself again, and for a moment Jenna didn't think she'd be able to continue.

"But what I really wanted to say today is that I loved him—*really* loved him. And I know a lot of you did too. I have to believe that counts for something. I think it's true what they say . . . that love never dies."

With that Dana could no longer hold back her tears, and Hank hurried over to guide her to a seat beside Kurt's family. Tears streamed down Jenna's face too. She slipped her hand into Peter's and he squeezed it reassuringly, but Jenna could tell he was struggling to keep from crying himself.

Then Coach Davis took the microphone. As he relived the highlights of Kurt's football career in his booming coach's voice, Jenna let her mind wander. Miguel had joined their group after all, she saw now. He stood silently behind Leah, his arms crossed, his expression stony. *He must have found us during Dana's speech*, Jenna realized. But instead of the little rush of excitement she usually felt at the sight of Miguel, all she felt was relief that Leah had been wrong. After the way Miguel had supported Kurt at the carnival, what in the world could have made Leah think he wouldn't come to Kurt's service?

Coach Davis wrapped up and yielded the podium to Principal Kelly, who seemed determined to do for Kurt's academic career what the coach had done for his athletic one. Jenna knew that the two men were only trying to make something uplifting out of Kurt's achievements, but their words were starting to have exactly the opposite effect on her. The more she heard about Kurt's great potential, the harder it was for her to understand why his life had been cut short. Of all the people at school, why had *Kurt* died? He probably had more people praying for him every day than any one of them.

Jenna shook her head and reached up to touch her

189

cross, the metal cool between her fingers. Yesterday she'd read her Bible and prayed with her parents late into the night, until she'd finally begun to accept what had happened. But she still didn't understand it.

The last of Kurt's family members stepped down off the dais, and Nicole wiped surreptitiously at the tears running out from under her sunglasses. Their speeches had been heartrending. She was glad the memorial was over.

When Jesse and Melanie had first joined the group, Nicole had thought she wouldn't be able to concentrate on a single word. She was furious with Courtney for bailing out on her and making her go to the service alone. But halfway through Dana's short tribute, Nicole had forgotten about everything else. Listening to Dana speak of love—of *true* love—made what she had felt for Jesse seem as small as the rest of her life.

The huge memorial crowd was breaking up and drifting apart, but the eight former members of Team Take-out seemed frozen in position, all lost in their separate thoughts. *This is it*, Nicole realized suddenly. *This is the last time this group will ever be together*. The thought made her sadder than she would have expected. *Just one more thing to be depressed about*.

"I feel awful," she said, breaking the silence at last. Heads nodded around the group.

"You know what the worst thing is?" Ben asked. "The worst thing is that it's over."

Nicole shook her head emphatically. "No way. I don't think I could have stood it if those speeches had been any longer."

"Not the memorial," said Ben. "The hope. Two weeks ago we didn't even know each other, but we came together to try to help Kurt, and for a while there, it felt like we'd really accomplished something. Now we know we didn't. That's the worst thing, I think. Knowing that it's over and we didn't make a difference."

Nicole stared at Ben, amazed. That was the most intelligent thing she'd heard for days—she couldn't believe whose mouth it had just come out of.

"Yeah. I know what you mean," Jesse said thoughtfully.

Nicole winced, annoyed to have agreed with Jesse, even by accident.

"Sorry, but I don't," said Peter. "I think we *did* make a difference. Not the difference we *wanted* to make, I'll grant you that, but aren't you glad now that we had the chance to do that one last thing for Kurt? His family appreciated it, and so did he. I've got to believe he's going to heaven with a great big smile on his face, just thinking about all the people who loved him. Kurt had faith . . . and so should we."

"Still," said Leah, a little skeptically, "I think we all know what Ben means."

Peter rubbed his jaw thoughtfully. "Maybe. But maybe it *isn't* over."

"What do you mean?" asked Nicole. "Of course it is."

"Not if we don't want it to be. Ben said he wanted to make a difference for Kurt, and I think I know a way we can do that."

"How?" Ben asked.

"Let's do something to honor Kurt's memory. Let's not *let* it be over."

"What could *we* do?" Melanie asked.

"Well . . . I don't have anything particular in mind—"

"Oh! I do!" Jenna interrupted excitedly. "Peter, what about the bus? The bus for the Junior Explorers?" Jenna's eyes shone as she broke into the first truly happy smile Nicole had seen all day. "We could do fund-raisers to earn a new bus for the kids, and then donate it in Kurt's memory!"

"What kids?" Leah asked.

"What *bus?*" asked Melanie, turning to Peter. "I didn't see a bus."

"That's because the old one died," Jenna explained before Peter could reply. "The city was supposed to pay for a new one, but they went back on their promise and now the kids won't be able to go on trips or to camp or *anywhere.*"

192

"That's horrible!" Melanie said. "They can't do that."

"I'm afraid they already did," Peter told her. "But Jenna, a bus costs a lot of money. I was thinking a little smaller, like maybe a scholarship prize."

"Oh."

Jenna looked so deflated that Nicole felt sorry for her. "It was a good idea, though," she said, reaching to pat Jenna's arm.

"Thanks."

The group stood there a moment in silence. It seemed there was nothing left to say but good-bye.

"I'll do it," Melanie said suddenly. "I don't care how long it takes."

"You will?" Jenna asked excitedly.

"Me too," said Ben with a wry grin. "I can probably wedge it into my social schedule somehow."

There was a brief, charged silence.

"Well, if everyone else is going to do it, I guess I might as well do it too," Jesse said grudgingly. Nicole couldn't help noticing he looked right at Melanie when he said it.

"Not to be difficult," Leah broke in, "but what exactly are Junior Explorers?"

Peter hurried to answer. "The Junior Explorers are some kids I work with from disadvantaged families. Me and my partner, Chris, teach them games and crafts and have a good time with them. In the summer we do a free camp. If it wasn't for the

Explorers, most of these kids wouldn't be able to afford any of the things we do. I hate to sound like I'm pushing my own program, but it really is a worthy cause."

Leah thought for another few seconds. "Okay. Count me in."

"That's so great!" Jenna said. "Everyone's going to do it! Oh, wait. Miguel, what about you?"

Miguel shrugged. "Why not?"

"That's everyone!" Jenna crowed.

"Excuse me," Nicole protested, glancing sideways at Melanie and Jesse, "I didn't say I'd do it."

Jenna looked crushed. "You . . . but . . . I thought you said it was a good idea."

"It is. Only . . ." *How exactly should I put this?* she thought.

"Oh, come on, Nicole," said Leah. "Don't break up the group."

"Please, Nicole?" Peter added. "It won't be the same without you."

"I just—"

"Please?" Jenna begged.

"Oh . . . all right."

Nicole didn't even want to hear what Courtney was going to say when she found out her best friend had just signed up for probably a year's worth of fund-raisers with the God Squad.

Thirteen

"Leah! Hey, can I talk to you a minute?"

Leah was walking home after the memorial service when Miguel caught up with her at the edge of campus, driving alongside in the ugliest, most beat-up old clunker she'd ever seen. He coasted forward with one hand on the steering wheel, leaning across the passenger seat to shout through the open window.

"What about, Miguel?" she asked, still walking. "I'm not in the mood for your tantrums today."

Miguel grimaced. "Okay. I deserved that. That's what I wanted to talk about." He pulled the car over to the curb and jumped out, the motor still running as he trotted to her side. "Just wait a second, okay?"

Leah stopped and turned to face him, her finely arched eyebrows raised. "Miguel, this isn't going to work. You and I, I mean. The truth is, I don't much like your attitude. It looks like we'll be working together on this bus thing, so I guess we should get along, but that doesn't mean we have to be friends."

"Leah, please. Would you just let me explain?"

"Explain what, exactly?" she asked, crossing her arms.

Miguel stood in front of her on the sidewalk, clearly at a loss. His eyes searched hers, trying in vain to make a connection. Then, surprisingly, he smiled.

"You're a hard woman, Leah Rosenthal. Do you know that?"

"I am not," she said indignantly, amazed he would dare to criticize *her* after the way *he'd* acted the day before. "This relationship just isn't going to work and I don't want to drag it out. I'm practical, that's all."

"Yep. Practically the hardest woman I ever met." The late-afternoon sunshine picked up the whiteness of Miguel's teeth as his smile grew into a winning grin. "Come on, Leah. Give me a chance here. I only want to talk to you."

"You think you can smile and make it all better, don't you?" Leah accused. Her voice was firm, but inside she knew she was grasping at straws. The effect he was having on her all of a sudden was completely unexpected. Her pulse raced, and there was a funny hollow feeling up high in her chest, as if she'd forgotten to breathe. Leah had always known Miguel was cute, but she was finally beginning to understand why girls trailed him around campus like lost little puppies.

Miguel shrugged. "It's been known to work in the past," he admitted playfully. "You've got to use what you have, right?"

"I guess," said Leah, shaking her head.

"Come on, Leah," Miguel begged, suddenly serious again. "Just take a drive with me." He put a hand on her elbow and nudged her toward his car. "After that, if you still don't want to know me, I promise I'll leave you alone."

"Oh, all right," Leah said, relenting. "But this is really pointless." *I think*, she added silently, settling into the ancient, split vinyl passenger seat.

Miguel smiled at her as he ground the car into gear, but as soon as they were out driving on the main road, he grew silent.

Great, Leah thought, studying his darkening profile. *He's doing it again—he's going all moody on you. Leah Rosenthal, you're an idiot!* She watched covertly as his brows drew into their familiar scowl and his clear brown eyes seemed to look inward.

"I thought we'd go to the lake," he said suddenly, surprising her.

"The *lake*? You're kidding, right?"

Miguel threw a startled glance her way, then chuckled. "Nothing like that, I swear."

Leah glared suspiciously, but gradually relaxed as they drove along the deserted country roads to the lake. Late-afternoon shadows stretched out on the pavement, and trees and cows zipped past like scenes from some peculiarly uneventful slide show. The final section of road was dirt. Dust gave form to dirty sunbeams and billowed in through their open windows as Miguel stopped the car at the edge of the empty parking lot.

"Come on," he said, climbing out. "I'll show you my favorite spot." He walked off toward the edge of the lake without waiting for her reply.

Leah watched, annoyed, as he disappeared into the dust; then she jerked her door open and followed him through the grassy picnic area. He was down at the shore, skipping stones on the water, when she finally caught up.

"I'm not coming down there and getting my shoes all muddy," she told him irritably, glancing at the sandals she'd worn to Kurt's service. "I thought you wanted to *talk*."

Miguel threw a couple more stones, as if he hadn't heard her, then stood gazing out over the sparkling surface of the lake. "All right," he said at last, pointing down the shore. "Meet me on the rock."

Leah had been on the rock he pointed to before— all the kids had. In the summer, the broad, flat stone that jutted out into the water was a favorite swimming platform. But now it was fall, and the rock was deserted. Miguel squelched along the waterline toward it, his sneakers making obscene sounds in the mud, and with a sigh Leah followed a parallel course on the hard soil farther up the shore. The long rock extended well back into the beach, and Leah managed to step onto it without walking through the mud. She strode out to the very end, where Miguel stood waiting for her.

"Well?" she said.

The only answering sound was the lapping of tiny ripples against the mossy edges of the rock. Leah plopped down onto its hot, smooth surface and stretched her long legs out in front of her, smoothing her skirt down around them. "I'm waiting."

Miguel hesitated, then sank down beside her. "I know I've been acting a little weird lately," he began in a stiff voice, as if he'd been rehearsing.

"A little," Leah agreed dryly.

"I . . . I'm just not used to people asking me questions. You ask a lot of questions."

"Oh, no. You're not going to make this my fault!" Leah said, scooting around to face him. "I talk to people all the time without having them go off on me in the middle of the quad."

"Yeah, well, I'm sorry about that. I *don't* talk to people all the time. I . . . I don't like to give myself away that much. The funny thing is, somehow I got a reputation for being cool that way, so I guess I figured I could keep my thoughts to myself forever.

You know, guys don't *care* if you talk or not. Until I met you, the girls didn't much care either."

"That's because they're not thinking about what's in your head, Miguel. All they see is that nice, shiny package."

Miguel smiled. "You think my package is shiny?"

"Get to the point," Leah told him, embarrassed.

"If I'd just told you in the first place, things probably would have gone a lot smoother," he resumed apologetically. "But it's not something I like to talk about. I never talk about it, in fact."

"Talk about *what?*" Leah asked impatiently.

"My father. He died when I was fourteen." Miguel looked down at the rock and jabbed viciously at a pocket of sand with his finger. "I used to think if I didn't say anything, if I just kept it to myself, then life would go on like it always had. No one would pity me. No one would offer useless sympathy. I thought it would be easier that way . . . and maybe it was. For a while."

"Oh, Miguel," Leah said quietly. "I'm so sorry."

Miguel shrugged. "Yeah, well, so am I, but it doesn't bring him back."

"How did it happen?"

"Cancer. He knew there was something wrong with him, but he didn't go to the doctor. We didn't have any health insurance."

Miguel paused and swallowed hard, his expression a mixture of pain and anger. "He kept working and putting off seeing a doctor, and by the time he finally collapsed, he was terminal. That was the first time any of the rest of us even found out he was sick."

Leah's heart ached for Miguel—both for what had happened and for the incredible burden of keeping it all inside. "I can imagine how awful that must have been."

Miguel snorted. "I doubt it. I doubt you've ever seen anyone die in that much pain. Screaming for the drugs . . . praying for death . . ." He shuddered, as if to shake off the recollection.

"Kurt and I were pretty tight once," he said, changing the subject. "We were altar boys together. I'll bet you find that hard to believe."

She found it shocking, actually, but she didn't want to say so.

"Kurt knew my dad. He knew the whole story, but he never told anyone at school. You could trust him that way. To keep a secret, I mean."

Leah nodded silently.

"You know, for a while there I think I had some dumb idea that I wasn't just helping Kurt—I was helping my father somehow. Like I could make it up to him by doing for Kurt what I should have done for my dad. I can't believe I was so stupid."

"I don't think that's stupid at all."

Miguel looked at her and their eyes connected

for a moment before he turned his head away again. "It must have been. Kurt's dead, isn't he?"

"Yes, but—"

"That's the way God works, I think," Miguel said bitterly. "They say the Lord gives and the Lord takes away, but it seems to me like he mostly takes away." He found a pebble in the sand and side-armed it out across the water.

"Is that why you quit going to church?"

Miguel nodded. Then he closed his eyes. Leah watched, amazed, as the tears slid down his cheeks like slowly melting ice.

"It almost killed my mother," he said when he could look at her again. "But being a faithful Catholic didn't save my father. How can I worship a god who'd kill a good man? Who'd kill him like *that*? And now Kurt . . ." He wiped angrily at more tears. "This is so embarrassing. Don't tell anyone."

"I won't." Leah put both her arms around him, desperate to soothe him somehow. "You can trust me."

The moisture on Miguel's cheeks glinted in the final rays of daylight as he nodded an acknowledgment. Barely realizing what she was doing, Leah leaned forward and kissed his cheekbones, tasting the salt on her lips. Miguel closed his eyes again. His thick black lashes made wet arcs on his tan cheeks. Leah hesitated only a moment before she kissed those tears away, too, her lips barely grazing his face. She could feel their hearts beating together, pounding faster every second. She held him more tightly, breathing in the scents of shampoo and chlorine, soap, and the warm, musky smell of his skin.

"Miguel?"

"Hmm?"

Slowly, tenderly, Leah lowered her lips to his and kissed him on the mouth.

"So, I guess I'll see you at that meeting at Peter's house tomorrow," Jesse said, his car idling in Melanie's driveway. "If I don't see you at school first, I mean."

Melanie nodded. Before Team Take-out had broken up, they'd all agreed to meet at Peter's house on Thursday night to plan their first fund-raiser. She let herself out of the BMW and slammed its passenger door.

"Thanks for the ride, Jesse. I don't think I could have faced the bus today."

Jesse beamed. "Anytime. You know that."

"Yeah, well, thanks." Melanie shouldered her backpack and walked into her house without a backward glance. But once she'd entered the dim interior, the raw gray concrete of the massive walls was oppressive. The silence was palpable, absolute. "Dad?" she called. No answer.

He's probably passed out in the poolhouse again, she thought. Over the last couple of days, he'd started to like drinking in the poolhouse even more than drinking in the den. Melanie dropped her backpack onto the floor, suddenly too tired to even climb the stairs.

She and Jesse had stayed at school to hang out with the team after the service, and outside it was just starting to get dark. The shadows crept through the living room and spilled across her shoes, filling her with despair. Here she was in her perfect cheerleader's uniform in her modern, palatial home, completely and utterly alone—Melanie Andrews, the toast of CCHS. What a joke. Melanie remembered the huge crowd of people who had cared about Kurt and she felt even worse—too depressed even to cry.

The sound of an engine revving in the driveway took Melanie by surprise. Jesse hadn't left yet! Impulsively, she spun around and threw her front door open, running out into the twilight to catch him before he got away. "Hey! Could you stay awhile?" she called. "I could order a pizza or something."

Jesse looked amazed, but happily so. "Uh, sure. Okay." He parked the car and climbed out, peering curiously through Melanie's open front door at what he could see of the house.

"You'd better come in before you get neck strain," Melanie said dryly, walking by him into the entryway. Jesse followed, right on her heels. She took him into the kitchen and switched on the overhead lights, then picked up a cordless telephone. "What do you want on your pizza?"

"Anything," Jesse answered distractedly, looking around the kitchen. "Man, this place is deluxe."

"Too bad no one knows how to cook." Melanie hit the speed-dial button for the pizza place and ordered a large pepperoni pizza with extra cheese. Then, still on the phone, she opened the refrigerator to see if she needed to add some Cokes. The enormous icebox was loaded with at least a case and a half of beer, but there were plenty of soft drinks, too, and even a few groceries. Her father must have sent Mrs. Murphy to the store. "That's it—just the pizza," she confirmed, hanging up the phone.

Jesse had settled onto one of the barstools behind the breakfast bar. "Do you want something to drink?" she asked him.

"Yeah. How about a beer?" He smiled rakishly, obviously thinking his remark very clever.

Melanie knew her dad would never know the difference, but she was in no mood to encourage Jesse's bad habits. She grabbed a Coke out of the refrigerator and tossed it across the kitchen to him, spiraling the can like a football. Jesse caught it easily.

"Stay here a minute, all right?" she said. "I just have to check on something outside." She slipped out the back door and hurried to the poolhouse. Sure enough, the low murmur of the television was audible through the door. She opened it just enough to see her father snoring on the sofa with his beer cans, then quietly shut it again. He wouldn't be bothering them tonight.

Walking back toward the house, Melanie felt a stab of annoyance. She was sick of the way her father had copped out on her. Her mother couldn't help leaving her—that was an accident—but her father had abandoned her voluntarily. Melanie's annoyance flashed into anger as she reached the patio again. Her mother had made her a kid with one parent—her *father* had made her an orphan. The moment she stepped back into the kitchen, Melanie knew what she was going to do.

"Hey, Jesse, I just thought of something you can help me with. You're a strong guy, right?"

Jesse smiled. "I like to think so."

"Great. I need help carrying a few things in from the garage."

"No problem." He chugged down the rest of his Coke, then slid off the barstool. "Let's go."

That was the point where she could have backed out. It would have been easy then to say "never mind." But she didn't. Instead she turned and walked through the house toward the adjoining garage, flipping on lights as she went.

"Could you hurry up?" she asked Jesse, who was following at a snail's pace and rubbernecking as he went. "I'd like to get there today."

206

"This is an incredible house." He seemed particularly fascinated by the bare expanses of rough gray wall, but every open doorway produced another excuse to slow down.

"It used to be." Melanie reached the garage door and opened it at last. Her father's tiny roadster looked lost in the enormous space, parked in the spot it was rarely moved from.

"Geez!" Jesse exclaimed behind her. "I thought *our* garage was big! You could park about fifteen cars in here."

"Ten," Melanie corrected. "My parents used to collect them. Before . . . you know. Afterward, my dad couldn't stand to look at them, and he sold all but the one he drives."

"Man, I'd have liked to see them." Jesse's voice was disappointed.

Melanie shrugged and started across the cold concrete floor to the locked door of the storage room. "I'll show you something else he couldn't stand to look at." She lifted the combination padlock and rotated the individual tumblers to spell out the morbid combination her father had chosen—the day, month, and year of her mother's death. The last tumbler clicked into place and the lock released. Holding her breath, Melanie opened the door.

"No one's been in here for almost two years," she told Jesse, hesitating in the doorway. Her voice sounded awed even to her own ears. She stepped forward and found a switch, blinking in the sudden light. Her mother's framed paintings crowded the specially built, carpeted racks in the climate-controlled storeroom, each of them placed on edge in its assigned slot like a book on a library shelf. Only the edges of the frames were visible, and there were so many of them that Melanie was overcome by the sight. She stepped forward and ran her fingers over the nearest one, the sharp remembrance of what she'd lost bitter in her throat.

"Whoa!" said Jesse. "What's with the art gallery?"

"These are my mother's paintings." Melanie tossed her hair to hide the emotion she felt. "I was hoping you could help me hang a few up."

Jesse shrugged. "Sure. Which ones?"

It was a good question. How could she ever choose?

"Well, this one, for starters." She pointed to the frame she'd been touching, not even sure which painting it was. "You take this big one and I'll grab a smaller one."

"Deal." Jesse reached for the painting and yanked it halfway out of its slot in one fluid motion.

"Careful!" Melanie cried. He froze. With the painting half exposed now, she could see that it was one of the peaceful, leafy landscapes her mother had excelled at. "I mean, careful, *please*. Could you put that in the living room?"

Jesse grinned and took off with the painting. The second he was gone, Melanie began pulling paintings out of their slots, searching, searching . . . she didn't even know for what. Each image spoke to her in a way it never had before. She had always loved her mother's paintings—had missed them intensely—but in the time they'd been put away, they seemed to have acquired a richness, a greater depth.

"I thought you were right behind me," Jesse complained, reappearing in the doorway.

"I got sidetracked," Melanie admitted. "Here, all of these I've pulled out need to go to the living room too."

Jesse seemed taken aback. "*All* of them? You said a *few*."

"That *is* a few," Melanie argued, gesturing to the many paintings still remaining in their slots.

"And where are you planning to hang them, anyway?" Jesse asked, not moving. "All the walls I've seen are concrete."

"No problem. You just need a special kind of nail." She left the storeroom and opened a tool cabinet in the garage, removing a big hammer and a box of heavy concrete nails. "See?"

Jesse's eyes widened when he saw them. "Those nails are going to make major holes. You'd better wait until your father gets home before you start using those in the living room. Where is he, anyway?"

"Um, out of town," Melanie lied, racking her brain for a decent alibi. "His, uh, his old company needed him for a special project."

"And he just left you here by yourself?" Jesse asked incredulously.

"I'm a big girl. Here, take these." She shoved the hammer and nails into Jesse's hands, then walked back into the storeroom and picked up two smaller paintings. "Come on."

In the living room, Melanie stood back and surveyed the pristine walls. After the pictures had been taken down and the old nails pulled, her father had had the concrete patched. The workman had done such a good job that Melanie hesitated now, uncertain where the old holes had been. She held a nail to the wall, then moved it back and forth, trying to find the spot. Her heart thudded erratically at the thought of actually hitting it with the hammer, and for a second she considered putting the paintings away and forgetting the whole thing.

Jesse seemed to sense her indecision. "Won't your dad be mad if you do this without permission?" he asked nervously.

"You have no idea," Melanie replied, an ironic smile curving her full lips. "He'll probably have a hemorrhage."

Then she picked a spot and started hammering.

"It's your funeral," Jesse muttered behind her.

Her first tentative blows only chipped the concrete as the nail skittered and bounced on the stony surface.

"You have to hit it harder," Jesse said.

"I know how to hit it," she retorted through gritted teeth. She pulled back the hammer and let one fly. The squarely struck nail bit deeply into the concrete. Another blow followed, then several more in quick succession.

"There," said Melanie, putting down the hammer. "Hand me that picture of the lake."

Jesse brought her the painting and helped loop its hanging wire over the nail. They both stood back to admire the finished result. "Hey, I recognize that spot," Jesse said slowly, staring at the watercolor. "I *like* that spot."

Melanie smiled, happier than she'd been for years. "Me too."

She'd driven two more nails and was hanging the third of the three paintings when the pizza arrived. "Get yourself something to drink out of the refrigerator," she told Jesse as she went to answer the door. "Bring me a Diet Coke, okay? And some extra napkins!" she shouted after him.

She paid for the pizza out of the spare cash her father always kept in the drawer of the entryway table, then spread out what napkins the delivery boy had given her on the marble floor, putting the greasy box on top of them. Jesse came back from the kitchen with more napkins and a couple of Cokes.

"Looks good," he said as Melanie lifted the lid and steam escaped from the pizza box.

She pulled two big slices out onto paper plates and handed one to Jesse. "Listen, I'm going to go get a couple more paintings. Eat your pizza—you're going to need your strength."

"For what?" he scoffed, taking a major bite. "Watching you drive three more nails?"

"You'll see."

Melanie set down her untouched plate and left the living room, a sneaky smile on her face. When she'd started the project, she really hadn't known how far she would take it. But somehow, sometime over the last half hour, her course had become crystal clear.

There were probably only fifty or sixty more paintings in the storeroom. If they put their minds to it, Melanie was pretty sure she and Jesse could hang them all by midnight.

Fourteen

Nicole rolled over in the Thursday-morning sunshine, feeling as if someone had hit her with a baseball bat. She'd been crying off and on for three days, and now all that grief had transformed itself into the worst headache of her life. Dull and pounding, it made the room spin around her as she sat up in bed and blinked in the light streaming through her window.

"Oh, my head," she groaned. It seemed cruel that the weather outside was so beautiful when all over town people were feeling almost as awful as she was. Almost—because they hadn't lost Jesse Jones on top of everything else.

"Ouch," she whimpered. The mere thought of Jesse made her temples throb double-time. All through the night Nicole had tossed and turned, worrying about her decision to join the fund-raising group at Peter's house and wondering if she ought to back out. All she had to do was pick up the phone and call Courtney—her friend would have a million excuses.

But the more Nicole thought about it, the more she didn't want to back out. It wasn't as if Jesse and Melanie were going to fall off the face of the earth. Unfortunately. No matter what she did, she'd still run into them at school. Meanwhile, she really liked Leah and Jenna, and Peter was nice too. Ben . . . was Ben. But Miguel was normal. Besides, she'd already given her word.

I'll go to the meeting, Nicole decided. She still wasn't sure if she was going in spite of Jesse or because of him, but suddenly it didn't matter anymore. Kurt's death had made her realize that there were other people in the world—people who could use her help. And it had made her realize something far less pleasant too: for a long time the only person Nicole had wanted to help was herself.

"I'm going to change," she vowed quietly, sitting up straighter in bed. And then she had an idea. Closing her eyes, she said a silent prayer, her whole heart in her words.

Dear God, I know I don't think about you as much as I should, or pray enough, or pay attention in church, but if you really know everything then you know how hard it is to be a teenager. Please watch over Kurt Englbehrt and his family, and please help us earn that bus for the kids. Oh, and God? I don't want to be shallow. Please help me remember that life is bigger than parties and clothes and diets and dates and . . . well, you know. All that stuff I like.

Melanie leaned against the kitchen counter and sipped her orange juice distractedly, worried she'd gone too far. When she and Jesse had first started hanging her mother's paintings the night before, she had only intended to hang a few—just two or three to let her father know she was mad at him. But when she'd seen them all there in the storeroom—when she'd run her hand over their frames—this wild, defiant feeling had come over her, like nothing she'd ever felt before. Now, in the harsh, cold light of morning, Melanie was pretty sure she'd gone temporarily insane. If her father ever came out of the poolhouse again, he was going to have a heart attack.

She walked around the breakfast bar and stuck her head into the living room, unable to believe what she'd done. Her mother's colorful paintings blanketed the once bare walls, reaching two stories high in the entry hall. Sometime after eleven o'clock she'd helped Jesse bring in the big metal ladder to hang those. And the strangest thing was, once she'd gotten started she'd seemed to remember exactly where each painting went. She'd hung them almost by instinct, faster and faster as the night wore on. There had been only one significant moment of hesitation, and that had been at the very end, when she'd stood in the doorway of her parents' bedroom with her mother's framed self-portrait clutched in sweating hands.

"Maybe you ought to leave your dad's room out of it," Jesse had advised, yawning, still clueless. "I mean, if he doesn't like the paintings . . ."

That had decided it, of course. The self-portrait went up, and so did the series of seasonal skies and an enormous meadow scene. When Jesse finally said good night and stumbled sleepily out to his BMW, the storeroom was empty. Melanie picked up their pizza mess and put the tools back in the garage. Then she wandered slowly through the house, soaking up the paintings. She was completely exhausted, mentally and physically, but for the first time in a long time, she was strangely at peace with herself. When she'd finally gone to bed, she'd slept like a little girl.

This morning, the fact that she'd slept at all seemed like some sort of miracle. She stood there facing her mother's paintings, awed as they revealed their full depth of color in the growing light, and wondered where she'd found the courage. Everything seemed sun dappled, both inside and outside the frames. The real sunlight glinted across the hardness of real concrete, glass, and marble, while the painted light filtered through dense green leaves, sparkled from lakes, springs, and rivers, and lit banks of clouds as soft as summer.

"What are you looking at, Mel?" asked a groggy voice in the kitchen.

Melanie spun around wildly, slopping her juice. Her father had just come through the back door.

"Nothing."

"You're going to be late for school, aren't you?" He glanced at the clock on the oven. "What time do you have to leave?"

"In a minute." Melanie used the spilled juice as an excuse to hurry back toward the sink, away from the living room. She picked up a sponge, her heart thudding sickly. "Do you want some breakfast, Dad?" she offered, standing in his path and trying to delay the moment when he'd find out what she'd done. "I could make you some toast."

Mr. Andrews shook his shaggy head, his glassy eyes telling Melanie food was the last thing on his mind. "That's okay," he mumbled, shuffling past her. "You go on to school." Then, before she could say anything else, he walked through the kitchen and into the living room.

Melanie froze, waiting for the explosion. What would he do to her? Would he hate her now? She squeezed the sponge so hard it started dripping on her shoes; then she tossed it distractedly into the sink, the juice she'd spilled forgotten. *Any second now* . . . Melanie felt weak with anticipation.

But the explosion never came. The only sound from the living room was complete and utter silence.

Melanie cracked her knuckles one by one, something she hadn't done since grade school. What was he doing in there? Was he even still *in* there? Maybe he'd walked right through and up to his bedroom without noticing.

Yeah, right, she thought.

The suspense was killing her. Slowly, quietly, she crept forward to the doorway and peered into the living room. Her father stood transfixed on the marble floor in the exact center of the enormous space, his eyes on the walls of the two-story gallery Melanie had created. Tears streamed unheeded down his cheeks as he turned slowly in place, trying to take it all in.

Melanie froze in the doorway, unable to move—unable, almost, to breathe. She'd never seen her father cry before, not even after the accident. She'd expected outrage, a tongue-lashing, punishment, threats . . . anything but this.

Then her father finished his rotation. Melanie flinched as his eyes met hers.

"Your mother . . . ," he said, his voice half-strangled. "Your mother was the most talented . . . the most beautiful person I've ever known. I . . . I ought to thank you for reminding me."

Melanie watched, speechless, as he turned and stumbled up the stairs. The moment he reached the top, she snatched her backpack off a stool and bolted out the front door. She didn't want to be home when he saw what she'd done to his bedroom.

Jenna was wedged in next to Peter on the Altmanns' living room love seat, but she didn't mind the lack of space. She could barely wait for the meeting to begin.

"Okay," Peter said, gesturing for everyone to be quiet. "Let's get started."

The group gradually stopped talking, and Jenna took the opportunity to smile at Miguel, who sat opposite her on the sofa, next to Leah and Ben. Melanie perched languidly on one of its arms, and Jesse occupied the stuffed armchair next to her. Nicole had come in last—she sat rather stiffly on a wooden chair Mr. Altmann had carried in from the dining room.

Peter's parents are being so great about this, Jenna thought. Not that it was any surprise. Still, Mr. Altmann had already come in and offered to help the group in any way he could, and Mrs. Altmann had baked them a batch of cookies. Jenna chewed at the end of her pen excitedly. Maybe they could have the next meeting at her house.

"Okay. Well, here we are," Peter began awkwardly. Jenna could tell he was nervous. "I guess we all know what the goal is, right? We want to buy that bus for the Junior Explorers." The others nodded in agreement.

"Right, then." Peter sat back slightly. "We'll need to start looking around for a good used bus we can buy, but we already know it's going to cost a lot of money. In the meantime, I think we ought to start some fund-raisers—get the cash coming in."

"It seems to me like the *first* thing we ought to do is figure out where we're going to put that cash," Leah said. "I vote that we kick in ten dollars each and open a savings account. Then we'll have a place to put our money and we'll always know exactly how much we've got."

"Good idea," said Melanie. "We ought to elect one person to be in charge of the money, though. I nominate Peter."

"Second," Jenna called quickly, happy to see her friend get the honor. "All in favor?"

The group answered with a unanimous "Aye."

Peter was flushed, but clearly pleased. "Well, if you all think so . . ."

"If Peter is going to be treasurer, then what about a president? And a vice president? And a secretary?" Jesse asked.

"There are only eight of us," Nicole protested. "You make it sound like we're starting a club or something."

"I don't mind taking notes, if you guys want me to," Jenna volunteered. She held up the steno pad and neon pink pen she'd brought along. "I was going to anyway."

"You ought to write down that the group is opening a bank account," Ben said, leaning forward from his place next to Leah. Something about the way Ben said "the group" gave Jenna an idea.

"We should have a name," she said. "We can't go around calling ourselves 'the group' all the time."

"What kind of name?" Melanie asked.

"I don't know," Jenna admitted. "I just this minute thought of it. How about . . . how about New Beginnings?"

Melanie made a face. "I don't get it. What's that mean?"

"Well . . . just that . . . something ended when Kurt died. But, in a way, now we're starting over again in his memory. Kurt's life ended, but our coming together to form this group is sort of a new beginning." Jenna glanced around the living room. The rest of the group seemed unconvinced.

"More like a beginning and an *ending*," said Nicole. "I only signed up for this until we earn that bus for the kids. That's what you all said, remember?"

Miguel and Leah nodded. So did Melanie.

"Maybe we should pick something a little more temporary-sounding," Leah suggested. "I think Nicole is saying we have more of a pact than a club."

"Exactly!" Nicole agreed, with obvious relief.

Jenna nodded. She still liked New Beginnings, but

she wanted everyone to be happy. "Okay. Then . . . how about CYA, for Christian Youth Association?"

Jesse snorted derisively. "I always thought CYA stood for cover your—"

"Never mind!" Jenna interrupted quickly.

"And anyway," Miguel protested, his voice annoyed, "who said anything about this being a Christian group? Leah isn't Christian."

"Neither am I," Melanie added quickly, before Jenna could respond. "I mean, don't get me wrong, I don't have anything *against* it. But I didn't think . . . I didn't realize you all wanted this to be a church thing." She slid off the sofa arm and onto her feet, hesitating awkwardly. "I guess I don't belong here."

Jesse stood up beside her. "I'll go with you."

"Wait! That wasn't what I meant at all," Jenna pleaded, wishing she'd never mentioned the subject of a name. She rose to her feet too, and so did Peter. "Melanie, please stay. I'm sorry. I wasn't thinking."

"I think it's just the type of project this is that made Jenna suggest that name," Peter explained, putting an arm around Jenna's shoulders. "Christians are supposed to help people, so it seems like a Christian project to us. We didn't mean to imply that everyone else has to believe what we do." Jenna couldn't help noticing the way he had shifted the blame from her onto both of them, and she smiled at her friend gratefully.

"It doesn't bother *me*," Ben piped up from the couch. "I'm a Christian."

Jesse shot him a withering look. "So am I, Ben. That's not the point."

Melanie wheeled to face Jesse, the surprise on her face apparent. She held his eyes disbelievingly.

Jesse squirmed, his normally cocky expression nowhere to be seen. "I don't go to church very often," he muttered.

"Anyway, you don't have to be Christian to do a good deed," Miguel grumbled from the couch. "That's ridiculous."

"No, of course not," Jenna agreed immediately. "I'm really sorry, Melanie. Leah, you too. Please don't go."

"It doesn't bother *me*," Leah replied. "I don't have a problem with religion." For some reason, she looked at Miguel as she said it.

"I don't have a problem with it either," Melanie clarified. "I just . . . don't believe it." She lowered herself slowly back onto the sofa arm, apparently deciding to stay.

Jenna flashed her one last apologetic smile before she and Peter sat down too. Jesse seemed to suddenly realize he was the last one standing. "All right, then," he said importantly, taking his seat as if he'd been the one to settle everything.

Unexpectedly, Melanie grinned. "When you think about it," she said, "it's actually kind of weird

223

that we met each other at all. I mean, we really don't have a whole lot in common."

"It was Kurt who did it," said Nicole. "None of us would be here right now if it weren't for him."

"I would. I live here," Peter joked.

"No, Nicole's right," Leah said. "This group feels more like something we were chosen for than something the eight of us chose." She smiled. "I guess you could call us Fate's Eight."

"Or how about Eight Mates?" said Miguel. Leah looked askance at him. "I mean mates like in Australia. You know—buddies. It's not . . . oh, forget it."

"I think we should call ourselves the *Great* Eight." That suggestion came from Jesse.

"Eight Friends," Jenna suggested, scribbling crazily.

"That doesn't rhyme," Peter told her.

"No, but it's nice." Jenna consulted her pad, then looked at Nicole. "How about you, Nicole? You haven't suggested a name yet."

"If *all* our meetings take this long, we'll be calling ourselves the No-Dates Eight," Nicole grumbled. She seemed genuinely surprised when the rest of the group erupted into laughter. Slowly, shyly, a smile crept over her face too.

"Why don't we just settle on The Eight?" Melanie suggested. "That's the part everyone seems to agree on."

There were scattered nods around the group, and the decision seemed to have been made, when Ben suddenly sat straight up. "I've got it! Eight Prime!"

"Huh?" said Nicole.

"A prime number is a number that can't be divided," Ben explained. "It can only be divided by itself. Well, by itself or by one—but when you divide eight by one, you still have eight."

"Eight isn't a prime number," Leah pointed out. "It divides evenly by two, or by four—"

"But that's why we'll be Eight *Prime*," Ben insisted. "We'll *make* it a prime number. We'll be the eight who can't be divided. You know . . ." He leapt to his feet, put his hand over his heart, and assumed a goofy, mock-solemn expression. "One number, indivisible, with liberty and justice for all."

"I like it," said Jenna, laughing.

Melanie said she liked it too, and Peter and Miguel nodded their approval.

"It's the perfect name," Leah decided. "It shows that we're committed. No one can divide us but us."

Ben beamed as if she'd just knighted him. He reclaimed his seat on the couch with such an excess of dignity that Jenna had to struggle not to laugh.

"It's fine with me," Jesse said, leaning back into his chair. "I always knew I was prime."

Melanie rolled her eyes, but everyone else laughed appreciatively.

Jenna's pen hovered over her pad. "Eight Prime?" she asked.

"Eight Prime!" the group agreed. Jenna wrote down the name with a flourish.

"I have an idea for the first fund-raiser, too," Ben said immediately.

"You're really on a roll, aren't you?" Miguel teased from Leah's other side. "Don't use yourself up the first night."

Ben blushed but pressed ahead. "A car wash. It's easy and it doesn't cost much money to put on. We could even do it this Saturday. It's supposed to be sunny all weekend, so getting wet won't matter."

"Good idea," said Peter.

"What about the Junior Explorers?" Jenna asked. "How are you going to wash cars and meet with them, too?"

"I think it will be great if they help us. I know they'll probably be more trouble than help, but I want everyone to meet them. Besides, it will be good for them to do something to help earn this bus—they'll appreciate it more that way."

"Having all those cute little kids with us won't hurt when we're trying to get people to stop, either," Melanie pointed out.

"Yeah, and that way we'll get Chris to help, too," said Peter. "And probably Maura, if we ask her."

A moment later everyone was shouting out things the group would need, followed by offers to bring them. Soap, buckets, hoses, towels, and signs were all accounted for quickly, and Nicole even offered to bring her dad's old cash box and some starter change.

"Wow, that seems like everything," Peter said. "I guess the only thing left is to decide the location."

Jenna looked up from her pad again. "We ought to have it at the park. Only not in the middle, where you usually meet the kids. Over at the edge, next to the boulevard. That way we can flag cars into the parking lot and wash them right there."

"It sounds good to *me*," Peter said, looking around the group for comments. No one objected. "I guess that's it, then. Boy, that was easy."

Jenna dropped her pen and shook her hand rapidly, trying to ease her writer's cramp. "I hereby move we adjourn the first official meeting of Eight Prime and eat all Mrs. Altmann's cookies," she said, the grin on her face contagious.

"Second!" seven different voices exclaimed in unison.

Jenna watched happily from Peter's living room window as the other members of Eight Prime trailed down his front walkway toward their cars. Melanie and Jesse were the first to drive off, Jesse at the wheel of his flashy red BMW. Nicole was right behind them, peeling out in the opposite direction a second later. Leah, Ben, and Miguel lingered, talking on the sidewalk on the opposite side of the street.

"It sure was a great meeting," Jenna said, her eyes on Miguel.

Behind her, Peter was picking up empty soda cans and rearranging the furniture. "Yeah. I can barely believe how well the whole thing came together. And I'll tell you what: the Junior Explorers are going to be *psyched* to see us all on Saturday."

"Mmm," Jenna agreed absently.

A car pulled up and Ben climbed in, waving to Leah and Miguel as he rode away. Jenna thought the man driving must be Mr. Pipkin, but she barely caught a glimpse of him before the car was gone. She turned her attention back to Miguel, still talking to Leah next to the beat-up old car that Jenna knew was his.

It was so amazing that they were going to be in this group together! Now she'd have all the time in the world to get to know Miguel, and hopefully someday to go out with him. Jenna crossed her fingers, keeping them in front of her so Peter wouldn't notice.

Miguel opened the passenger door of his car, and Jenna suddenly realized that he must have driven Leah to the meeting. Leah moved to get in, then stopped, still talking.

"What's so fascinating out there?" Peter asked.

"Huh? Nothing," Jenna said quickly, turning her back on the window.

"I'm going to take these dishes into the kitchen. Back in a minute."

She waited until Peter was safely out of the room, then turned around to check the window one last time.

Leah was standing behind the open passenger door now, her back to the car. Miguel leaned forward from the curb, a hand on the roof on either side of her. The smile on his face was lazy, playful, as he held Leah in his trap. Their bodies were almost touching; their faces were close together.

Too close, Jenna thought, feeling the first twinge of panic. *What are they doing?*

Then, as a horrified Jenna watched, Miguel lowered his face to Leah's and kissed her. Leah's arms circled Miguel's neck, pulling him closer, clinging possessively. They fit together perfectly, as if they were made for each other. The stolen kiss stretched on until tears blurred Jenna's vision.

No! This can't be happening! she thought, devastated. *Miguel and Leah. Why did it have to be* Leah? Jenna spun blindly away from the sight, everything reeling around her.

"Whoa! What's the matter, Jenna?" Peter was hurrying toward her, his familiar blue eyes telegraphing his concern from clear across the living room.

"Nothing!" she said, jumping away from the window. "Hey, Peter, let's go, uh, thank your mother for those cookies. Where is she? In the kitchen?" Jenna hustled him out of the living room, desperate to keep him from looking outside.

"She's in the den." Peter was staring as if she'd gone crazy.

"Even better. Let's go."

Peter shrugged, bewildered. "If you say so." He turned and walked toward the den. Jenna followed, blinking hard to keep back the tears.

Some new beginning this turned out to be, she thought miserably, fighting for control.

There was no way that what she'd just seen between Leah and Miguel had been a first kiss. *No* way. Somehow, somewhere, those two had become a couple—Jenna was sure of it. And now they were all going to be in Eight Prime together. Jenna could hardly imagine anything more awkward. The only thing that could have made it worse would have been if the group had known about her crush.

No one will ever, ever know how I feel about Miguel, she vowed silently, wiping roughly at tear-filled eyes.

I'll never tell anyone. Not even Peter.

About the Author

Laura Peyton Roberts holds an M.A. in English literature from San Diego State University. A native Californian, she lives with her husband in San Diego.

Read all about Jenna, Peter, Melanie, Ben, Leah, Miguel, Jesse, and Nicole in Clearwater Crossing #2, Reality Check

Peter watched Jenna surreptitiously as he helped Ben, Nicole, and Courtney wash an old Taurus. He'd managed to work next to her most of the day, but he didn't want to be too obvious about it. When Jenna had gone to help Maggie, Peter had decided it was a good idea to go his own way for a change.

"Hey, Peter," said Ben. "What are you doing tonight after the car wash?"

Peter jumped, startled. "Huh? Oh. I'm not sure, but I think I have plans," he answered vaguely.

Ben nodded, clearly disappointed, and Peter made a mental note to invite him to do something later. There was no way he was asking Ben to hang out with him tonight, though. Not if things turned out the way he hoped they would.

He glanced over at Jenna again. Even though he'd known her since sixth grade, lately it seemed as if Jenna looked slightly different every time he saw her. No matter how hard Peter tried to memorize her face, the picture wouldn't stay fixed in his mind. He'd think he had it one day at lunchtime; then that same night he'd find himself lying awake, futilely trying to recall a certain feature. Oh, sure, he could always imagine Jenna in a general way. But that wasn't good enough anymore. Peter wanted the details: the sun-streaked strands in her long brown hair, the dimples in her cheeks when she smiled, the four perfect freckles, the tiny, almost unnoticeable chip she'd put in one front tooth by falling off his skateboard.

It didn't take a genius to figure out what was going on, and Peter had finally admitted it to himself over the summer. He was in love.